THE OWL AND THE NIGHTINGALE
CLEANNESS
ST ERKENWALD

ADVISORY EDITOR: BETTY RADICE

The Owl and the Nightingale was written by an unknown author shortly after the death of Henry II (1189). The Bible epic *Cleanness* almost certainly, and the saint's legend *St Erkenwald* probably, were written by the north-western poet who composed *Sir Gawain and the Green Knight,* *Pearl* and *Patience,* the unknown master of English medieval alliterative poetry.

Brian Stone wrote his first book *Prisoner from Alamein* (with a foreword by Desmond MacCarthy) in 1944. After the war, during which he was decorated, he taught English in boys' schools for eleven years, and then trained teachers for ten years at Loughborough and Brighton. He has recently retired from the Open University where, as a founder member in 1969, he was Reader in Literature. His other translations in Penguin are *Sir Gawain and the Green Knight, Medieval English Verse,* and *Chaucer: Love Visions.* A fifth, of two fourteenth-century Morte Arthure poems, is in due to appear in 1988.

THE OWL AND THE NIGHTINGALE

❧

CLEANNESS

❧

ST ERKENWALD

TRANSLATED
AND INTRODUCED
BY
BRIAN STONE

Second Edition

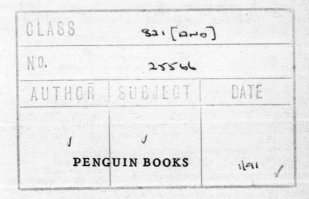

I DEDICATE THIS SECOND EDITION
TO THE MEMORY OF BETTY RADICE,
WHO COMMISSIONED THIS BOOK

PENGUIN BOOKS

Published by the Penguin Group
27 Wrights Lane, London W8 5TZ, England
Viking Penguin Inc., 40 West 23rd Street, New York, New York 10010, USA
Penguin Books Australia Ltd, Ringwood, Victoria, Australia
Penguin Books Canada Ltd, 2801 John Street, Markham, Ontario, Canada L3R 1B4
Penguin Books (NZ) Ltd, 182–190 Wairau Road, Auckland 10, New Zealand

Penguin Books Ltd, Registered Offices: Harmondsworth, Middlesex, England

Published in Penguin Books 1971
Reprinted 1977
Second edition 1988
Copyright © Brian Stone, 1971, 1988
All rights reserved

Set in Monotype Poliphilus
Revisions set by Merrion Letters, London

Made and printed in Great Britain by
Cox and Wyman Ltd, Reading

CONTENTS

FOREWORD

THESE three poems are examples of major genres of medieval religious writing: saint's legend, Bible epic, and religious debate. Each poem is based on a heritage of religious belief and practice, on a literary convention, and on history, to all of which I attempt to do justice in my separate introductory essays. These all begin with discussion of such cultural and background material, and conclude with literary analysis. Taken together, the essays will, I hope, give an insight into the age, and those on 'St Erkenwald' and 'Cleanness' are intended to help rescue these fine poems from comparative neglect. On 'The Owl and the Nightingale' a large body of work exists; I hope that my fresh critical approach to the poem will be accepted as an addition to it. I believe that close analysis of the structure and rhythm of each poem provides the key to its deepest meanings.

I wish to acknowledge a special debt to the editors of the texts upon which my work on the poems has been mainly based. For 'St Erkenwald' and 'Cleanness', I relied chiefly on the editions by Sir Israel Gollancz (EETS/Oxford, 1922 and 1921 respectively), and for the 1987 revisions I used Henry L. Savage's edition of 'St Erkenwald' (Yale UP, 1926) and A. C. Cawley and J. J. Anderson's edition of 'Cleanness' in *Pearl, Cleanness, Patience, Sir Gawain and the*

Green Knight (Dent, Everyman's Library, 1976). For my
work on 'The Owl and the Nightingale' I used the various
major editions: by J. E. Wells (1907), J. W. H. Atkins
(1922), Grattan and Sykes (1935) and E. G. Stanley
(1960). As the work progressed, I found that, more and
more, E. G. Stanley's appeared to be the one which was
most accurate and informative; and I came to rely on it
increasingly. If my immersion in the work of Gollancz and
Stanley has resulted in occasional failure to acknowledge a
particular thought or detail, I hope that this general and
unqualified acknowledgement will be acceptable. I also
owe a special debt to J. W. H. Atkins, not only for the
voluminous support material and the literal translation in
his 1922 edition of 'The Owl and the Nightingale', but for
the valuable insights into medieval ways of thinking provided in his *English Literary Criticism: The Medieval Phase*
(Methuen, 1943). I found the support material in John
Gardner's *The Complete Works of the Gawain-Poet* (University of Chicago Press, 1965) useful, but his translation of 'St
Erkenwald' and 'Cleanness' appeared to me to be idio-
syncratic in method (see pp. ii–xi of his Preface) and often
plainly wrong. I also wish to thank Oliver St John Gogarty
and Messrs Constable & Co. for the poem 'After Galen'
on p. 199, published in *The Collected Poems of Oliver St
John Gogarty*.

I gratefully acknowledge the help of my colleague, Dr H.
Francis Clark, without whose valuable comments and sug-
gestions my writing on religious matters, both in the introductory essays and in the notes to the poetry, would have
been more inaccurate and impoverished.

Readers may need to be reminded that the poems were all
composed for a literary audience whose culture was still pre-
dominantly an oral one. The texture of the poems is thus

largely open, and the style and the rhythms are, on the whole, beautifully and simply rhetorical: qualities I have tried to keep in my translations, which should be read aloud, if possible.

Kensington
July 1987

BRIAN STONE

ST ERKENWALD

(BISHOP OF LONDON 675–93)

—

An alliterative poem, written about 1386, narrating a miracle wrought by him in St Paul's cathedral.

INTRODUCTION

THIS poem belongs to a genre of writing which is central to the purposes and ceremonies of the medieval church: the saint's legend. Records of the sermons of the age, and of the instructions to the priesthood concerning the aims and contents of sermons, show clearly how legends and descriptions of the saints supplemented Bible stories and direct preaching. By extolling local and perhaps contemporary heroes and heroines of the Church, by emphasizing their holiness and especially their humanity, the preachers hoped to stir their congregations to emulation. When this sermon material came into literature under the scribal hands of those same preachers, people read, recited and sang its solemnities and marvels; and a huge corpus of work grew up. Thomas à Becket was the favourite saint of England in the Middle Ages, and the commonest subject of hagiologists, but to Erkenwald falls the distinction of having been the subject of the best saint's legend in English poetry. It is a compassionate devotional poem about the working of divine grace, and an *exemplum* of God's justice.

It is also a London poem of importance, in which the great city and its centre of worship become elements in the vision of a perfect Christian society. The rebuilding of the cathedral goes forward, the holy bishop brings grace and salvation to a scene threatened by supernatural disorder, and a whole town population fulfils its potential of blessedness. Thus, historically as well as poetically, both the saint and the work deserve attention; and perhaps the way to full appreciation may first be illuminated by history, both true and fanciful. The poet draws on two widely separated periods.

The first is the remote and fancifully chronicled time of the events described; this is the late seventh century, when Christianity was at last being consolidated in southern England, a period concerning which more conjecture than history survives. And the second is the late fourteenth century – possibly the actual year 1386, when Bishop Braybroke ordered St Erkenwald's two feast-days, 30 April and 14 November, to be celebrated once more as major festivals. Then, a sumptuous re-building of St Paul's cathedral was naturally followed by an outburst of special veneration of the city's first saint, in which the writing of this poem commemorating one of his miracles has fitting place.

Erkenwald was consecrated Bishop of London in about 675. The shadowy times before him yield some chronicle material which, since it was used by the poet, is given here, together with other evidence. Dean Ralph de Diceto (1180–1202) wrote of the beginnings of Christianity in Britain:[1]

Pope Eleutherius [of the second century] sent Fagan and Duvian, who baptised [the British] King Lucius, and transferred to the one God the dedication of the heathen temples. There were in Britain twenty-eight flamines and three arch-flamines, and these were replaced by bishops and archbishops. To the Archbishop of London were subject 'Loegria' – southern Britain – and Cornwall; to York, Northumbria and Scotland; to Caerleon, Wales.

This account, which remained the official one until the end of the Middle Ages, was largely erroneous, but odd details from history tend to suggest that London's Roman characteristics, given form by the tradition upon which Diceto drew, persisted well into the period of the Saxon invasions.

1. Quoted by W. R. Matthews and W. M. Atkins: *A History of St Paul's Cathedral* (J. Baker, 1957 p. 3.).

It is recorded that in 314 the Council of Arles was attended by Restitutus, Bishop of London. That is the only actual evidence that London was Christian under the Romans; the temple of Mithras unearthed in the City seems, from the available evidence, to have gone out of use in about the fourth century. The poet of 'St Erkenwald' probably drew on such an amalgam of tradition concerning the Roman use of the site of St Paul's as that offered by Dugdale:[2]

That in the place ... had been a temple of Diana the goddess, is probable enough from those instances the learned Camden giveth; viz. the structure near at hand, called Diana's chambers, and the multitude of ox-heads digged up, when the east part was re-builded (viz. temp. Ed. I),[3] which were then thought to be the relics of the Gentiles'[4] sacrifices; whereunto I shall add what I find in an ancient writer, viz. after that Christian religion, which in the days of King Lucius[5] had been first planted in this nation, was through that great persecution of Dioclesian[6] the emperor almost utterly rooted out, idols were set up in those churches where God had been served. ... London sacrificed to Diana, and Thorney (which is now called Westminster) to Apollo.

Sir Christopher Wren, while working on the new cathedral after the Great Fire of London (1666), found no evidence of pagan worship on the site.

2. Sir William Dugdale, Garter Principal King at Arms: *A History of St Paul's Cathedral*, (1658), with additions by H. Ellis, (1818).

3. Edward I, 1272–1307.

4. 'Gentiles' usually simply meant 'heathens'.

5. Lucius was never King of Britain, but, states Sir Mortimer Wheeler (*London and the Saxons*, London Museum Catalogue No. 6, 1935), of Britium, a Syriac word meaning 'castle'.

6. Dioclesian's persecution of the Christians started in 303.

It has been conjectured that, some time after the Romans left, the site of London became desolate, but at least we know that for forty years more London was in communica/tion with Rome, and that at no time, then or later, is there any record of London having been destroyed. Suggested evidence of the continued existence of a corporate city stead/ily resisting Saxon incursions, and retaining Romano–British characteristics, is provided by Sir Mortimer Wheeler,[7] who points out that more relics from 400–600 have been found in London than from 600–800; that Saxon burial/grounds in the Thames valley tend to be outside the London area; that the coins of the period found reflect the Roman preference for copper and gold rather than the Teutonic preference for silver; and that the positions of the so/called 'Grim's Dykes' support the foregoing evidence. Hence he suggests that there was a 'sub/Roman triangle' about the Thames estuary, with its points at Colchester and Canter/bury, and its apex to the west of London and St Albans. Subsequent archaeological work tends to confirm Sir Mortimer's view. So, according to this view, London be/came a refuge for Britons fleeing Saxon depredations and settlement on the south and east coasts, and retained some limited independence at the meeting/point of tribal areas based broadly on Essex, Wessex and Kent. Bede[8] notes that London was 'a trading centre for many nations who visit it by land and sea'.

That picture fits what we know of London when August/ine arrived in 597, with instructions from Pope Gregory that the Christianization of Britain should be based on two ecclesiastical centres, London and York; not the three of

7. Wheeler, op. cit.

8. Bede: *A History of the English Church and People*, 731, trans. by Leo Sherley/Price (Penguin, 1965), pp. 212–13.

London, York and Caerleon of the Celtic tradition, by which London was made one of the 'Triapolitan' cities (l. 31). Augustine found London 'resolutely pagan' (*New Catholic Encyclopaedia*) and withdrew to Canterbury; hence that city is the seat of the primate of all England today. London evidently had an international life of its own too strong for any tribal or religious group to absorb it permanently as yet, though many tried. Sir Mortimer, writing of the seventh century, summarizes pleasantly: 'A Kentish king builds a cathedral there, a Mercian sells its bishopric, a Wessex king speaks of a bishop of London as "my bishop".'[9]

It seems that the process of Christianization in London after St Augustine's arrival was roughly as follows:

Mellitus, Archbishop of Canterbury in 604, succeeded to the metropolitan see in 609, having been commanded to preach to the East Saxons. His king, Ethelbert of Kent, had built St Paul's, but after his death (616) and that of his nephew, Saebehrt, King of the East Saxons, both Kent and Essex returned to paganism. Mellitus fled or was banished to France, and the next bishop of London was the shadowy St Cedd (about 654), who re-converted the people of Essex. His name is connected with the Romanesque church at Bradwell-on-Sea. Cedd died at York, and of his successor, Wini, little is known, except that he was banished from Winchester by Kenewaltho, King of the West Saxons, was set up as Bishop of London by Wolfere, King of Mercia, and died in Winchester in about 671.

None of these three left any mark on London, but Erkenwald, who was Wini's successor and thus the fourth bishop of London, developed such historical and legendary importance in his lifetime that Bede, writing in 731, strongly attested his sanctity:[10]

9. Wheeler, op. cit., p. 92.   10. Bede, loc. cit.

For to this day the horse litter in which he travelled when ill is preserved by his disciples, and continues to cure many folk troubled by fever and other complaints. Sick people are cured when placed in or near the litter, and chips cut from it bring speedy relief when taken to the sick.

Another legend about Erkenwald, probably of twelfth-century origin, also centres on the missionary travelling for which the saint was famous, and of which the poet makes use ('Yes, Erkenwald was in Essex on an abbey visit' – l. 108):

During one of his journeys a wheel came off, but its fellow did its work so well that the car remained upright until the saint had reached his destination.'[11]

If the details of Erkenwald's life traditionally handed down are true, they evidence a profound religious respect on the part of the temporal rulers,[12] and saintly constancy of purpose and loftiness of aim on the part of Erkenwald himself. They are as follows:[13] Erkenwald, son of Offa, King of the East Angles, was born at Lindsey in about 630, and was thus about forty-five when he became Bishop of London. He was appointed by Theodore of Tarsus, a fiery and energetic old man who finally established Christianity in the areas which had recently lapsed into paganism, and was the first Archbishop of Canterbury to have full control of the English Church.

Erkenwald at once converted his patrimony – thus giving up all right to succession in the Kingdom of the East Angles – and with the proceeds set up two Benedictine foundations,

11. Matthews and Atkins, op. cit., p. 5.

12. Bede mentions with approval several kings, princes and nobles of his time who took monastic vows and gave up temporal rule.

13. Taken mainly from the *New Catholic Encyclopaedia* and the *Dictionary of National Biography*.

one at Chertsey, of which he became titular abbot, and the other at Barking, of which his sister Ethelburga, who was also canonized, became abbess. (Bede devotes several pages to the miracle-graced life of the Barking nuns.) Erkenwald enlarged St Paul's cathedral, added to its revenues, and obtained papal privileges for it. It is important to remember, in considering this kind of activity, that in those days, according to Matthews and Atkins, a bishop owned all church property in his diocese; he was accepted as the living authority of the patron saint, and his clergy were in fact his subjects. After a life of good works, in which his journeys in and about the bishopric were prominent, Erkenwald died at Barking Abbey on 30 April 693.

There were great strugglings ... after his death between the canons of St Paul's and the monks of Chertsey, both challenging the body to be buried with them; but in the meantime the people of London took away the body, and caused it to be buried in his own cathedral church, where it was interred in the nave: and afterwards, A.D. 1140 (but more solemnly, in 1148) translated, and laid in a very sumptuous shrine.[14]

As soon as Erkenwald was dead more legends gathered round his name. The very means by which the people of London had had their will over the disposal of his remains were declared miraculous, and a medieval hymn described him as 'the Light of London'. In the consolidation of Norman rule in the twelfth century the revival of native church traditions worked as cement: it was Bishop Robert de Sigillo who laid Erkenwald's remains 'in a very sumptuous shrine'. A life of St Erkenwald, and an account of his miracles, were written by one of Gilbert the Universal's nephews. The great work of re-building St Paul's began in the mid thir-

14. Dugdale, op. cit., p. 215.

teenth century, and went on for about a hundred years, until the time when the poem was written. It is first referred to as 'The New Work' (l. 38) in 1277, and in 1312

was the pavement of the New Work made of good and firm marble, which cost 5d. the foot. And within three years afterwards a great part of the spire of timber (covered with lead) being weak, and in danger of falling, was taken down, and a new cross, with a pomel well gilt, set on the top thereof; in which cross the relicks of divers saints were put ...'[15]

The poet builds upon contemporary interest in the re-building of the cathedral, adds the legends and partly-ascertained facts about pagan worship in the area, and welds them into a harmonious setting for the performance of the miracle by his hero. 'St Erkenwald' is a carefully worked artefact, based on an exact sense of the quintessence of medi-eval Christianity. Conversion, miracle, grace, warning of hell and celebration of heavenly bliss are smoothly packed into a swiftly-moving poetic narrative set in an archetypal Christian society. The whole thing could be recited on a public occasion as an interlude, or given as an edifying post-prandial entertainment before the company rose from the benches; twenty-five minutes of marvel, high drama, poetic finesse and impeccable doctrine.

There are three circles in the poem. The first is the great arena of historical England, the wider setting of the poem, in which the poet develops an idea of the importance of Lon-don, and prepares us in epic style for a momentous narration (ll. 1–32). It was a standard device of medieval writers to link the setting of their matter with the heroes of ancient history; the bogus attribution of the founding of Britain to the 'Trojan' Brutus, and the appellation 'New Troy' for London, were universally accepted.

15. Dugdale, op. cit., p. 11.

The second circle is the immediate environment in which the events of the poem happen, a recognizably medieval London, in which citizens of all degrees and many types take vigorous part in the action. There are 'merry masons' and 'pick-men in plenty' working in the foundations of the cathedral, and 'many masters' men of manifold occupations', including 'lads', who come running to the cathedral when news is spread of the discovery of the uncorrupted body in the tomb. Higher up the social scale, there are 'magistrates and messengers too', and of course 'the mayor and his muster'. When Erkenwald approaches, his herald is sent in advance, and in the celebration of the mass he is surrounded by 'ministrants'. Among the congregation are the nobility: the representation of society is just about complete in this first half of the poem (ll. 33–176). This London circle, which the Bishop enters rather late, after a suspense build-up of the kind we come to recognize in good drama, contracts until at its centre only the two protagonists are left.

Pagan corpse and holy man, in this third, circumscribed circle (ll. 177–340), at the tomb, work in their dialogue towards the fulfilment of the poet's aim, but the latter does not forget the audience of the second circle. They are all there, fully participating as well as looking on:

While the sepulchred man spoke, there sprang from the people
Not a word in all the world, nor awoke one sound;
As still as stones, all stood and listened,
With much wonder over-mastered, and many wept. (217–20)

And again, after the corpse's description of his agonized suffering in Limbo:

Thus dolefully the dead man described his anguish,
And all wept for woe at the words they heard. (309–10)

So that their joining in the rapture of the finale binds the newly-saved soul and the holy miracle-worker in an entire society. It is the perfection of the poet to give us a conclusion of only twelve lines: one stanza for the fantastic instant de-composition of the corpse, one for the complete doctrinal message, and one for the eruption of joyful worship and thanksgiving all over London.

It is not known whether the poet used an existing legend of St Erkenwald. The only antetype for the pagan judge appears to be the emperor Trajan (A.D. 53–117). According to a popular medieval legend this non-Christian just man reached heaven through the intercession of St Gregory. Dante deals with it, and St Thomas Aquinas mentions it. Gollancz discusses at length the poet's possible indebtedness to the legend.[16] But the miraculous preservation of corpses was common in medieval literature, and the poet may have been inspired by such stories. Bede in particular celebrates many holy men and women whose bodies resisted corrup-tion in the tomb: he relates, for example, that the body of St Cuthbert was found uncorrupted after eleven years in the tomb, with his clothes 'not only spotless, but wonderfully fresh and fair'.[17] By emphasizing these miracles Bede demon-strates the supernatural power of God to mark out the especially elect after death, and aims to further the faith by publishing them as widely as possible. But viewed another way, Bede is reflecting a fairly standard pagan belief: that the soul goes on inhabiting a corporeal frame, and that if the latter is preserved in some way, that is evidence that the gods have in fact preserved the soul. Orthodox medieval Christ-ian belief, by contrast, regarded the death and decay of the

16. Sir Israel Gollancz; *St Erkenwald* (EETS, Oxford, 1922), pp. xxxviii–li.

17. Bede, op. cit., p. 260.

physical body as natural concomitants of the elevation of the soul to bliss. And this is a point made with power by the poet.

The body of the pagan judge is indeed preserved in the tomb, but the preservation is a device which enables the poet to solve the problem of the pre-Christian good man. Normally such a person, being one of the just of the Old Testament, would have remained in Limbo until Christ's death and resurrection, and then been raised to heaven at the 'harrowing of hell'. The poet is being original in allowing a pagan unbeliever the same resurrectible status as a believer like, say, Abraham. In the light of the poet's insistence on the judge's rectitude (ll. 229–56), I read this as an interesting foreshadowing of the distinctly Protestant idea that one may be saved by works almost irrespective of one's faith. The judge has earned the right to be preserved until Christian times, when through the intercession of an anointed priest he may achieve his deserved eternity of bliss. And when this moment comes, no useful function remains for his body:

> With that he stopped speaking, and said no more.
> But suddenly his sweet face sank in and vanished,
> And all the beauty of his body blackened like mould,
> As foetid as fungus that flies up in powder.
>
> For as soon as the soul was established in bliss,
> That other lore was lost which made the corpse look alive;
> For the eternity of true life, which is utterly timeless,
> Makes void the vain glory that avails so little.   (341–8)

A characteristically medieval 'holy marvel' thus focuses attention on the relation between earthly good conduct and the immortality of the soul, making the latter the real consequence of the former in a slightly heterodox way.

The particular grace granted by God to the good pagan in the poem is treated as an exemplar of general application, and is won by a succession of means, each of which carefully embodies a Christian teaching point, even as it gives an enriching impetus to the narrative. Rarely does a didactic poet succeed in making such explicit recommendations about conduct and doctrine merely by narrative implication. It is done so unobtrusively, and so integrally with the narrative and the characterization, that one may easily miss the two important maxims in such a stanza as:

Word of the greater wonder after a while was brought
To the bishop, about the body buried so uncannily.
At the time he was travelling with his attendants in the provinces:
Yes, Erkenwald was in Essex on an abbey visit.   (105–8)

They are, I suppose: 'A good flock reports problems to its spiritual leader', and 'A good pastor visits his flock'. Tradition indeed attaches to Erkenwald the Celtic predilection for itinerant ministration, to which the Roman one for sound central episcopal administration was subsequently added. Many such incidental precepts figure in the poem.

The major doctrinal preoccupation of the poet is with the nature and power of prayer. When he first arrives at the scene of crisis, Erkenwald's first reaction is to shun everyone until strengthened by the right kind of intensive service:

The dark night dragged through till the daybell rang,
But Sir Erkenwald was up in the early dawn before,
Having wellnigh prayed all night at the canonical hours,
Beseeching his sovereign of his sweet grace
To vouchsafe him a vision, or reveal the truth otherwise.

(117–21)

Good prayer is hard work, and Erkenwald feels that he has been answered only after he has wept and groaned while praying. Mass in the cathedral follows, the corporate ceremony graced by 'delectable flights of melodious choiring'.

The scene is set for the second and final stage of the miracle – the first stage having been a thousand years before, when God determined that the dead man's body should be put in peculiar Limbo to await Christian redemption. So perfect is Erkenwald's state of mind and spirit that, when the time comes, he has no need to pray, but only to state his intention of praying, to cause the miracle. His overflowing compassion is all-sufficient, and a single tear brings about a mighty effect, in which a corpse disintegrates, a soul is saved, and a city rejoices.

In the end, in a narrative work, it is the characters which count. Of the two in this poem, Gollancz has the astonishing opinion that it is the pagan judge who is the hero. Although discussion of this question of priority might appear academic, it does lead to consideration of the total effect of the poem, which is likely to be gauged correctly if narrative and dramatic criteria are invoked as well as didactic ones. The latter offer a simple structure: an injustice (the languishing in Limbo of a good man) exists; a saint expunges it with divine aid. Ergo, the saint is the hero. If the criteria of, say, tragedy, are used, another structure emerges. A living, dead man is clogged with a terrible spiritual burden (non-possession of Christian grace); the chance of redemption comes; his innate virtue enables him to take it; he dies happy. Change being the vital principle of dramatic development, the pagan judge must be the hero, because he is the one who is changed. He was in a state of conflict amounting almost to despair; he is now spiritually entire, and in bliss. The question is, what change is it the main purpose of the writer to convey, and by what means does he set about it? After all, if only theological criteria were adduced, God would be the only possible hero of the poem.

The change, the resolution of the problem presented, may

perhaps best be examined by considering the two characters as they are at first described, and as they come together. They are provided with characteristic settings of nicely contrasted utility and vividness. That of the bishop is the bustling living world, in which his first manifestations are right actions, purposefully decided on and carried out:

[He] ... at once on his white horse came swiftly home.   (112)

But he passed into his palace, impressing peace upon them,
Kept away from the corpse, and closed the door behind him.
(115–16)

He behaves throughout with the uncomplex certainty of tranquil virtue.

The setting of the pagan judge is one of mystery in which his antique sarcophagus, his miraculous preservation and his enigmatic stillness together compose the essence of what he is: the embodiment of terrifying, supernatural latency.

That kind of contrast is kept up throughout, until all contrasts are dissolved by that single, wonderful tear. Erkenwald is of this world, the pagan is of another. Erkenwald's world is firm, structured and predictable; even things which seem enigmatic can be resolved by right prayer and action. The pagan's world is entirely of the spirit, shifting and dominated by the unpredictability of injustice: he refers to his soul

Deeply pining in the dark death doomed by our father,
Our ancestor Adam, who ate of the apple,
And poisoned perpetually a people quite guiltless.   (293–6)

How could a dispensation which he recognizes as ideal condemn him to such anguish for ever?

Erkenwald is at peace within himself, and suffers only for others; that suffering, on the pagan's behalf, is proof that Erkenwald has achieved the fourth of C. S. Lewis's Loves, what Lewis calls Divine Gift-Love, which enables man 'to love what is not naturally lovable; lepers, criminals, enemies, morons, the sulky, the superior and the sneering'[18] – and, by extension, pagans. The pagan, on the other hand, has no insight into others, except to yearn for whatever peace the saved soul may enjoy; he is an utter abstract of personal spiritual suffering:

> Long may my soul sit in sorrow, sighing wretchedly
> In the dimness of dark death, where day never dawns,
> Famished in the fiendish pit, yearning for food.   (305–8)

It is good to consider the resolution of the poem at the moment when the pagan character is extinguished, and to see it simultaneously on three levels: the supernal, the terrestrial, and the infernal. On earth the tear falls; in heaven the vibration of the liquid landing liberates the ever-potential grace; in Limbo

> A gleaming light flashes low in the abyss.

For a moment, action is suspended, while the (now former) pagan expatiates upon what has happened, for the benefit of his human hearers; and then time resumes. The sweet face sinks in and rots like fungus, the people lament the departed and rejoice that his soul is saved, and sounding church bells proclaim a new miracle and glory to God. The hero–saint is left in possession of the field and the flock, radically changed as he must be by the light which the living and the dead have shared for a moment.

18. C. S. Lewis: *The Four Loves* (Fontana, 1969), p. 117.

ST ERKENWALD

Prologue

At London in England not a long time after
Christ suffered on the cross and established Christendom,
The city had a saintly and sanctified bishop;
And it happened that Erkenwald was the holy man's name.

In the town at that time the temple most eminent
Was partly pulled down and purified by dedication,
Having been heathen in the days of Hengist,[1]
Whom the savage Saxons had sent over here.

They beat out the Britons, pushed them back into Wales,
And poisoned the piety of the people everywhere:
Recreant to God was the realm for many rank years,[2]
Till St Augustine was sent to Sandwich by the Pope.

He preached the pure faith and implanted the truth here,
Brought the body corporate back to Christianity,
And the temples which at the time pertained to the Devil,
He cleansed in the name of Christ and called churches.

1. Hengist and Horsa were invited to settle on the Isle of Thanet by the Celtic king Vortigern, who was looking for allies. From the pan-Celtic point of view, like 'Diarmuid and Dervorgilla, who brought the Norman in' to Ireland, he shall 'never be forgiven'. W. B. Yeats: 'The Dreaming of the Bones', *Collected Plays* (Macmillan, 1952).

2. Bede censures the native British, the Celts, for not trying to convert the invading Saxons.

He hurled out their idols, brought in saints,
Furnished them more fittingly and freshly named them.
What had been Apollo's previously, was St Peter's now,[3]
What Mahomet's was St Margaret's or Magdalen's church.[4]

The synagogue of the sun was made sacred to Our Lady,[5]
And Jupiter and Juno's fane to Jesus or to James.
All the seats of Satan in Saxon times
He established for splendid saints, and sanctified and
    hallowed them.

What is now named London was known as New Troy,[6]
The metropolis and master-town in that time as now;
Its mighty minster was a monstrous fiend's domain,
And the title of the temple was taken from his name.[7]

For he was held the highest of all idols worshipped,
His sacrifices the most solemn under Saxon sway.
In the Triapolitan towns, this temple was one of three:[8]
Within all Britain's borders, there were but two others.

3. This may be a reference to Westminster Abbey, which was
founded by Saebehrt, King of the East Saxons.

4. The reference is thought to be to St Margaret's, Westminster.

5. 'Synagogue' in Middle English was used to describe any
heathen temple. Probably the identifications in this stanza were
determined by alliterative needs.

6. 'Trinovantum' (Latin) = 'Troy Novant' (Old French) =
New Troy.

7. The name of the Saxon deity is not given. Although tradition placed the worship of Diana on the site of St Paul's, the worship of Mercury would better have suited Hengist, who told
Vortigern that his god was Woden, god of traffickers and mer-
chantmen.

8. Triapolitan. See Introduction, p. 17.

I

Under Augustine's authority, Erkenwald was now bishop
Of beloved London town, the Law's teacher,
And splendidly placed on St Paul's minster throne,
A temple of the Triapolitan, as I told you before.

Next it was razed to ruin, but rose up afresh
In a noble and noteworthy labour, known as the New
  Work.[9]
Many a merry mason was made to work there,
Hewing the hard stone with well-honed tools,

With pick-men in plenty to probe the ground,
So that from the first the foundation should be firmly based;
And as they mightily dug and mined, a marvel came to
  light,
As the chroniclers with their craft recorded for our memory.

For as they dug and delved so deeply into the ground,
They found in the floor a wonderfully fashioned tomb,
A sarcophagus curiously carved from Cyclopean stones,
Graced with gargoyles, all in grey marble.

The canopy of the coffin, covering it on top,[10]
Was finely fashioned of marble finished most smoothly,
And the border was embellished with bright gold letters:
Mysterious they stood, in sentences arcane.

Most clear were the characters the crowd gazed upon,
But all were unable to utter their meaning.

9. The New Work. See Introduction, p. 20.

10. I follow Gollancz's guess about this line which is so
clouded in the manuscript, not Savage's suggestion that Craigie's
reconstruction be followed (see Savage, op. cit., pp. 27-8).

Wise men with wide foreheads, wondering in that pit,
Struggled without success to string them into words.

When tidings of the tomb-wonder were taken to the town,
Hundreds of high-ranking men hastened there at once;
Magistrates and messengers made their way there,
And many masters' men of manifold occupations.

Lads left their labour and leaped to the place
In a rapidly running rout ringing with sound.
Such a crowd of all kinds came there eagerly,
Like all the world's dwellers swarming there at once.

When the mayor and his muster had surveyed the marvel,
With the sacristan's assent, they sealed off the holy place
And ordered the lid to be lifted off and laid at the side:
They were longing to look at what lay in the coffin.

Forthwith, brisk workmen went to it with a will,
Put levers to the lid, lifting it from underneath,
Caught up the corners with crowbars of iron,
And large as the lid was, they levered it off quickly.

Then perplexity in plenty came to the people standing there,
Who could not comprehend that curious marvel:
Gleaming and glittering in gold paint was the interior,
And on the bottom lay a body of blissful appearance,

Arrayed in noble raiment, in a regal style.
In glistening gold his gown was hemmed,
With many a precious pearl placed upon it;
And a girdle of gold gripped his waist.

He wore a mighty mantle, miniver-trimmed,
Made of excellent camel hair edged fittingly;

A coruscating crown on his coif was placed,[11]
And a splendid sceptre was set in his hand.

Neither spot nor stain soiled his garments,
Which were not mouldy or marked or moth-eaten,
But so bright and brilliant in their beautiful colours! –
Yes, as if but yesterday in the Yard they'd been tailored.[12]

And as fresh were the face and the flesh elsewhere naked –
The ears and the hands openly showing
With rich ruddiness of the rose, and two red lips –
As if in sound health he had suddenly slipped into sleep.

They wasted time wondering, one to another,
Whose body it might be that was buried there;
How long he had lain there, his look unchanged,
His attire still all unstained. So men speculated as follows:

'The memory of such a man as this must have remained.
He was king of this country, as clearly appears
From his lying dug so deeply down: indeed it would be odd
If no account in a chronicle recorded his existence.'

But nothing noteworthy came of it, for none could discover
From any sign, or inscription, or story even,
Recorded in Britain's chronicle, or an account in a book,
That mention was ever made of such a man at all.[13]

11. A coif was a closed hood worn by senior lawmen such as
Chaucer's Man of Law.

12. The 'Yard' is St Paul's churchyard, a traditional place for
business. Gollancz notes that Bishop Braybroke in 1385 acted
against people who traded within the cathedral itself, but that
tradition gives the date 1587 for the first erection of shops in the
Yard. Stationers and printers collected there.

13. The expectation that the solution to the problem might be
found in a book is typically medieval.

Word of the great wonder after a while was brought
To the bishop, about the body buried so uncannily.
At the time he was travelling with his attendants in the
    provinces:
Yes, Erkenwald was in Essex on an abbey visit.

Men told him the whole tale, and of the tension among the
    people,
The outcry about the corpse which clamoured on and on.
To halt it, he sent heralds, and afterwards, letters,
Then at once on his white horse came swiftly home.

When he came to the cathedral called after St Paul
On his mare, many met him with the marvel on their lips,
But he passed into his palace, impressing peace upon them,
Kept away from the corpse, and closed the door behind him.

The dark night dragged through till the daybell rang,
But Sir Erkenwald was up in the early dawn before:
Nearly all night he had knelt in prayer,
Beseeching his sovereign of his sweet grace
To vouchsafe him a vision, or reveal the truth otherwise.

'I know well my unworthiness' was the weeping prayer
Of his humble honesty: 'Hear me, O Lord!
To confirm the Christian faith, help me fully to explain
The mystery of this marvel that amazes the people.'

His groaning prayer for grace was granted at last:
The Holy Ghost answered, and afterwards day broke.
The minster doors were ceremonially opened for matins to be
    sung,
And the saintly man prepared solemnly to sing high mass.

The prelate was arrayed promptly in episcopal robes,
And began the mass with his ministrants in mannerly dig-
nity.
Sweetly singing Spiritus Domini, that success might follow
The delectable flights of melodious choiring.

Many grandly dressed great lords were gathered to hear it
(For the courtliest in the kingdom often came there to wor-
ship),
And stayed till the service ended, said were the amens,
And the priests in due process had paced from the altar.

The nobility bowed to the bishop as he passed them;
Then he turned towards the tomb attired in his splendour.
With a clattering of keys the enclosure was unlocked,
While the people, much perplexed, thickly pressed behind
him.

The bishop came to the burial-place with barons beside
him,
The mayor with many mighty men, and mace-bearers before
him.
The sacristan of the splendid place told the story in detail
Of the finding of that fearful wonder: with his finger he
pointed.

'My lords,' he said, 'Look! here lies a body
Which has lain here below for how long none knows,
Yet no decay in the clothing or its colours appears,
No fault in the flesh or the fine coffin he lies in.

'Nobody alive was living so long ago
That his mind has memory of such a man ruling,

Or knowledge of his name or noteworthy accomplishments,
Yet plenty of poor people are put in graves here
Whose memory is immortally marked in our death-lists.

'And we have looked in our library for a long seven days,
But no chronicle of this king has come to our notice.
He has not lain here so long, to look by the light of nature,
As to melt out of memory, unless a miracle accounts for it.'

'Well spoken!' then said the sanctified bishop,
'But what is miracle to man amounts to little
If put by the prescience of the Prince of Paradise,
When it delights him to unloose the least of his powers.

'When man's might is mastered, his mind overcome,
His senses destroyed, and he stands confounded,
God lightly lets loose with his littlest finger
What all the hands under heaven could never hold.

'When mankind with his craft and counsel goes astray,
The creature must recover in the Creator's strength.

To our work then at once, and wonder no more:
Seeking the truth by ourselves you see is useless.
Let us call on the Creator and crave the grace
Of him who widely grants wisdom to waft us his strength.

'And to make fast your faith and further its purity,
I shall teach you truly the extent of his powers,
That at length you may believe him to be Lord Almighty,
And set to serve your desires if you esteem him friend.'14

14. The peroration of Part I of the poem serves a triple purpose.
It gives a dramatic pause, it foreshadows the meaning of the coming action, and it develops suspense.

II

Then he turned to the tomb and talked to the corpse,
Lifting up its eyelids and letting loose these words:
'Now, corpse in this coffin, keep quiet no longer,
Since Jesus has judged that his joy shall be shown today.

'Obey therefore his behest, I bid you on his behalf!
As he was broken on a beam when his blood was shed –
And well you are aware of it, and we believe it too –
Respond to what I say, and conceal nothing from us!

'Since we are ignorant who you are, inform us yourself
What you were in this world, and why you lie thus,
How long you have lain here, what religion you practise,
And whether you are bound for bliss or banished to
    damnation.'

When the saintly man had spoken, sighing as he ended,
The marvel in the mausoleum moved a little,
And with a sad and dreary sound said these words,
Helped by some heavenly spirit from him who rules all.

'Bishop,' said the body, 'your bidding is precious to me:
I would not be barred from bowing to it for both my eyes.
The high name you have uttered and held me to answer
Commands all heaven and hell, and earth between.

'First concerning myself, let me say who I was:
As unhappy an inhabitant as earth ever had,
I was no king or kaiser or courteous knight,
But a lawyer in the legal system this land then used.

'I was commissioned and made a master of the judges,
To give counsel on weighty causes and control the city
Under a prince of proud lineage of the pagan law;
And each liegeman he led believed the same religion.

'How long I have lain here would be a labour to state;
No mortal mouth could make the date clear.
Almost eight hundred years, all but eighteen,
After Brutus in the beginning built this city –

'Three hundred and fifty-four years in fact
Before, by the Christian account, Christ was born, –[15]
In New Troy I was itinerant judge travelling in oyer[16]
In the reign of the royal monarch who ruled us then,

'The bold Breton Sir Belin – Sir Brennius was his brother.
Many an angry insult was offered between them,
Various the violent wars while their vengeance lasted.
I was appointed principal judge here of the pagan law.'

While the sepulchred man spoke, there sprang from the
    people
Not a word in all the world, nor awoke one sound;
As still as stones, they all stood and listened,
With much wonder over-mastered, and many wept.

The bishop ordered the body, 'Lay bare the reason why,
Since you were king of no country, the crown is on your
    head;

15. This tortuous dating gives 1136 B.C. for the foundation of
London, and 354 B.C. for the supposed misgovernment of Belinus
and Brennius. But the sources the poet used in fact state that
Belinus began to reign 354 years after the founding of Rome.
    16. 'oyer'. Short for a court of 'oyer et determiner' = to hear
and determine, the action of dispensing summary justice.

How you hold so high in your hand the sceptre,
When land and life and limb of liegemen were not yours.'

'Dread sir,' the dead man said, 'I do affirm
It came about quite contrary to my wish.
I was deputy and doomsman under a duke of rank,
And this place was completely put in my power.

'I kept my courts fairly in this comely city,
Even in the forms of good faith, for more than forty winters.
False-hearted and fierce were the people, refractory to rule,
And I often received hurts in my efforts to keep them
    virtuous.

'But never in weal or woe, wild rage or dread,
For awe of any man, or influence, or bribes,
Did I deviate from right, as I deemed it,
To settle a case deceitfully on a single occasion.

'My conscience never cringed before covetousness on earth,
To deceive by serving up a spurious judgement,
For reverence of a rich man, a ranking noble,
Or menaces from men, or malice, or pity.

'None deceived me into swerving off the straight road of
    right,
For I comported myself as perfectly as a pagan can.
I would offer no evil judgement to him who had killed my
    father,
Nor false favour to my father, though it befell him to be
    hanged.

'Since I was honest and upright and expert in the law,
On the day of my death a doleful din was heard in Troy.
All grieved at my going, the great and the humble,
And in their bounty they buried my body in gold;

'They clad me in the finest clothes the courts possessed,
In a mantle meet for the most humane of judges,
Robed me as if I were the richest ruler in Troy,
Befurred me as befits one of flawless faith.[17]

'In honour of my honesty and its high renown,
They crowned me and declared me king of clever justices
Enthroned in Troy, thinking me without equal;
And as I ever held to the right, they offered me the sceptre.'

The bishop searched further still, suffering in spirit,
And asked how, though men honoured him highly,
His attire was still untarnished. 'Into tatters, surely,
It should have rotted, and been rent into rags long since?

'Your body may be embalmed: I am barely surprised
That it is not crumbled with rot or rank with worms,
But the colouring of your clothes! I cannot understand
By human lore how its lustre has lasted so long.'

'No, Bishop,' said the body, 'embalmed I never was,
Nor was my clothing kept immaculate by mankind's
    wisdom,
But by the ruler of reason who recommends justice,
And loyally loves all the laws of truth;

'Who more honours men for remembering justice
Than for any other earthly action of merit.
And if mortals so mantled me for maintaining right,
The Lord who most loves right has allowed me to last.'

17. In matters of faith, as those of rank, the apparel should proclaim the man.

'Yes, but speak of your soul now,' then said the bishop.
'Where is it set and established, after so straight a life?
He who pays each for his actions accordingly
Would hardly forgo the giving you his grace in some
   measure.

'For it is stated in the Psalms, where he speaks his truth,
"The righteous and uncorrupted shall rise to my abode".[18]
So say of your soul where it resides in bliss,
Of God, how he granted you this great restoration.'

The man lying there murmured, moved his head,
Gave a great groan, and gasped out to God,
'Mighty maker of men, your mastery is great!
How may your mercy ever be manifest to me?

'Was I not a heathen ignorant of your holy nature,
The measure of your mercy and your mighty virtue?
A fellow without faith, defective in the law
In which, Lord, you were worshipped? Woe the hard
   time!

'I was missing among the many whom your misery re-
   deemed
With the blood of your body on the black cross.
When you harrowed the pit of hell and haled them out,
All lifting you praise from Limbo, you left me there.

'And my soul still stays there, and cannot see out of it,
Deeply pining in the dark death doomed by our father,
Our ancestor Adam, who ate of the apple,
And poisoned perpetually a people quite guiltless.

18. Presumably a reference to Psalm xxiv, 3-4: 'Who shall
ascend into the hill of the Lord? or who shall stand in his holy
place? He that hath clean hands, and a pure heart.'

'You were tainted by Adam's teeth and so turned venomous'
But then recovered through the cure that constitutes your
  life –
Fair baptism in the font, in full faith,
Which myself and my soul, starved of mercy, missed.

'To what advantage was our virtue so valiant for justice,
When we are dreadfully condemned to the deep chasm,
And sundered from that supper, that solemn feast,[19]
Where honour is offered those who hungered after righteous-
  ness?

'Long may my soul sit in sorrow, sighing wretchedly
In the dimness of dark death, where day never dawns,
Famished in the fiendish pit, yearning for food,
Before seeing that supper, or being received at it!'

Thus dolefully the dead man described his anguish,
And all wept for woe at the words they heard.
The bishop lowered his eyelids in lamentation,
And sobbed without ceasing, and so could not speak.

But he took his time, then towards the tomb he gazed
At the body laid so low, through his flowing tears.
'May Our Lord allow that your life return,' said he,
'By the grace of God, when I get holy water,

'And cast it on the fair corpse, declaring as I do so:
"I baptize you in the name of the Father and his fair Son,

---

19. The 'solemn feast' is a metaphor for eternal bliss, derived
ultimately from the parable of the marriage of the king's son in
Matthew xxii.

And of the gracious Holy Ghost". And the words gone –
  enough!
Then if you drop down dead, it does me no harm.'[20]

As the words went forth, from his watering eyes
The tears trickled down and touched the tomb.
One fell on the face, and the fair body sighed,
Then said most solemnly, 'Our Saviour be praised!

'Now may you, the high God, and your gracious mother,
  be given praise,
And blessed be the blissful hour she bore you.
And may you be blessed, Bishop, who banished my grief,
And relieved my soul from the loathsome gloom of her life!

'For the sentence you spoke, and the sprinkling of water,
The bright brook of your tears, brought about my baptism:
The first drop that fell finished all my woe.
Now my soul may be seated at the supper table.

'For with the words and the water that wash away pain,
A gleaming light flashed low in the abyss,
So that my spirit sprang swiftly with unstinted joy
To the feast where all the faithful feed in fine solemnity.

'And there a marshal met her with matchless ceremony
And appointed her a permanent place with reverence.
So I hallow my high God, and also you, Bishop;
Blessed may you be, bringing us bliss from anguish!'

With that he stopped speaking, and said no more.
But suddenly his sweet face sank in and vanished,
And all the beauty of his body blackened like mould,
As foetid as fungus that flies up in powder.

20. Erkenwald is well aware of the consequence of his proposed
action. If the pagan dies, Erkenwald will have saved his soul.

For as soon as the soul was established in bliss,
That other lore was lost which made the corpse look alive;
For the eternity of true life, which is utterly timeless,
Makes void the vain glory that avails so little.

Then loftily Our Lord was praised, with uplifting of hands,
Much mourning and merriment mingled together;
Then they paced forth in procession, the people following,
And all the bells in the city bounds boomed out together.

CLEANNESS

INTRODUCTION

CLEANNESS is a Bible epic poem in 1812 lines, in which three main and several minor stories from the Bible or religious tradition are used to illustrate the theme of that cleanness, or purity, recommended in the Sixth Beatitude: 'Blessed are the pure in heart; for they shall see God' (Matthew, v. 8). Its versified form is:

> Fair shall befall the fully pure in heart:
> They shall look on our Lord, and be blithe in spirit.
>
> (27–8)

By 'cleanness' the poet means two related things: one is purity of life, especially in sexual matters, and the other is loyal service to God. All three Bible stories, the Flood (ll. 193–556), the Destruction of Sodom and Gomorrah (ll. 557–1156) and Belshazzar's Feast (ll. 1157–1812), concern the misdeeds and fate of sinners who failed in both respects. Each story is prodigiously expanded from the Bible account, in harmony with the poet's narrative and descriptive eloquence, and with his precise doctrinal purpose. Whereas early English versifiers of parts of the Bible had tended chiefly to inject grandiose verbosity into their subject, and so to destroy the forceful sublimity of the original, this poet transmutes his material, yet in making his own artefact from it remains true to the Bible. His transmutations are: to give poetic form to holy writ; to expand the detail with a wealth of concrete imagining, especially in his descriptions and characterizations; to provide the reader with a doctrinal commentary; and to reinforce this commentary, both with illustrations from other parts of the Bible and with direct homiletic teaching. Above all, by his selection, description

47

and teaching, he isolates one important quality inherent in the Bible, and treats it in depth.

The poem is in fact a single homily on a grand scale, containing three main *exempla* which provide the structure, just as the three circles I define in 'St Erkenwald' (see p. 20–21) make the frame on which that poem is built. In the Flood, the whole world is drowned on account of its sin; in Sodom and Gomorrah, an evil nation in a low valley is swallowed up in hell; in Babylon, a vicious royal family with its noble hangers-on is slaughtered. As the stories succeed each other God becomes more discriminate in his vengeance, and the sins he punishes more and more specifically violate his sacraments. At the same time, in the interspersed homilies, as the nature of the sins is defined and the punishment of the sinners is held up as dreadful warning, so the beatific vision and the means by which it may be had are kept before the reader. The central homily (ll. 1049–1156), which links the story of the Destruction of Sodom and Gomorrah with that of Belshazzar's Feast, places the essential Christian cynosure, the person of Christ the Pearl of God, at the heart of the poem. In Christ is found the highest kind of cleanness, the quality which, above all others, binds Man in sacrament[1] to God.

The nature of this sacrament is peculiarly medieval, carrying as it does elements which belong definably to the concepts of feudalism and courtly love; rank, the granting of obedience and honour to the earthly or heavenly master, absolute politeness and courtly ceremony, are seen to be attributes of the divine pattern which are unquestioningly harmonized with Bible precept. They operate through the cleanness which gives the power to the sacrament, and which is freshly defined in connection with each story. The

1. I use the word in its wider application.

structure of each episode, whether major or minor, has the following general features:

At the outset, the courteous and holy sacrament between Man and God is defined. Then the nature of erring man is lamentingly expatiated upon:

> The mind of man is inclined mostly to evil, (518)

and the breaking of the sacrament by a particular man or group of people is described. God expresses his anger, wrestles with it, and decides, usually in dialogue with a just man who still holds to his sacraments, what conjunction of vengeance and mercy he will exercise in the case. The punishment follows, always with tremendously powerful and graphic descriptions. The moral is drawn, the pure soul which contrasts with the punished sinners is described, and the episode concludes with the promise, and sometimes the description, of the beatific vision that the pure in heart will enjoy.

In reading and interpreting the Bible priestly scholars naturally wished to find that the Word of God expressed a unified and comprehensive message, to which each of the sixty-four books made a harmonious contribution. But often discovering instead obscurity and even contradiction, they early concluded that God spoke in riddles, and devised means to make matters plain and to reconcile differences. The poet followed the standard practice of medieval exegesis in allowing himself to understand and interpret holy writ in four ways.[2] The first was the *literal* or *historical* sense, which

2. For a general discussion of these, see G. R. Owst: *Literature and the Pulpit in Medieval England* (Blackwell, 1961), ch. 2, 'Scripture and Allegory', pp. 56–109. And for this poet's use of them, John Gardner: *The Complete Works of the Gawain–Poet* (University of Chicago Press, 1965), pp. 31–7. I am indebted to both.

gave the straightforward meaning. The second was the *allegorical* sense, which offered an interpretation connected with faith or doctrine, and cannot always be separated with certainty from the next two senses. The third was the *anagogical* sense, which invited the devout scholar to see what he was reading as representing something else, especially something leading up to a heavenly reality: prophecies, other events, and particularly, if the subject was in the Old Testament, to see it as anagogical of something in the New. And the fourth and last sense was the *tropological*, which placed the matter in relation to an entire religious scheme of things in which the object was to define the progress of the soul in the estate of God. Having such freedom of interpretation the medieval scholar could take himself and his readers very far from the Bible if he employed excessive ingenuity and imagination in the service of his devotion. But if the modern reader is prepared to move into the generally symbolic mode accepted in the Middle Ages, he will not find it hard to read 'Cleanness' with an appropriate consciousness, for the poet has a constant sense of his theme, which his four scholastic uses of his Biblical material are disciplined to serve.

The Prologue (ll. 1–192). Cleanness is defined, and the Parable of the Marriage Feast typifies the way in which God works to attract pure Man to heaven. The punishment of the man without a wedding garment is not to be understood literally, as this would make the host of the parable, and hence God, appear monstrously cruel; but allegorically. Throughout the poem, brightness and cleanness of raiment stand for a pure condition of soul, and the man is rightly punished because his tattered clothes show him to be both disloyal and impure. The wrath of the host is justified because he offered an incomparably luxurious feast (ll. 55–60), publicized its availability, and indicated the conditions on which it was to be had; three actions symbolizing essential elements in a successful compact between Man and God. Man has to recognize the beatific vision and to take positive action to obtain it; if he takes the wrong action, being one of the chosen who yet refuse to serve God, then his punishment is the more severe:

Their badness is more blameworthy than blind Gentile sin.

(76)

The poet explains all this in the homiletic conclusion to the Prologue (ll. 161–92), where his culminating statement, after which he lists the examples of unclean life abhorrent to God, is

Without doubt the deeds you have done are your clothes, (171)

A short bridging passage (ll. 193–248) concerning God's vengeance on Lucifer, and on Adam, follows. It has two purposes. The homiletic aim is to show the reader that, in two famous cases of disloyalty, God mitigated his wrath. The artistic purpose is to take the reader into the early world in which sin first occurred and Man took up his destiny; and in this early world, with its potentiality for anagogical interpretation – for surely even Old Testament Jerusalem and Babylon, the scenes of the third great episode of the poem, seem ancient compared to the world of the New Testament – the poem remains.

The Flood (ll. 248–555). The sin of lechery committed by the generation of Noah is seen as the begetter of all other sins. First of all, it is an outrage of nature to plant human seed elsewhere than in the proper container, the womb: following the account in Genesis, the poet expresses the mystical idea that the seed is a holy essence which transmits God's plans for Man in due form from generation to generation. And if the seed is not used in the right way, being either squandered or misplaced as the result of lustful mating of unsuited kinds (ll. 269–72), then all other evils follow:

> Love of slaughter was their sign of distinction,
> And the one whose wickedness was worst was called best.
>
> (275–6)

The ark symbolizes the Virgin Mary, who is the 'container' of the infant Christ, just as the ark is the container which keeps the uncorrupted creation safe above the heaving waters of God's wrath. The poet uses the same word for both containers, but does not otherwise make the comparison explicit.

In the Parable of the Marriage Feast, and in the short accounts of the punishment of Lucifer and Adam, the poet has shown both that God did become angry, and what happened when he did. But here, in the story of Noah, nothing is so merely expository and retrospective; we are shown God goaded by the vivid cause, woundingly perplexed in his wrath; hurt inwardly, as it were, by the sin and ingratitude of Man. His turning to Noah (l. 301) prefigures his later turning to Christ, who will make possible both the redemption of Man and the restoration of the harmony of God. There is a powerful anthropomorphism at work here, and elsewhere in the poem.

The moment of redemption in the Noah story is nicely summarized by John Gardner:[3]

In identifying as symbolically one the salvation of man and Nature by Noah, and the salvation of the ark by the dove, the poet has brilliantly fused courtesy of three kinds, divine, human and natural.

God's promise never again to destroy his creation marks his

3. op. cit., p. 66.

acceptance of the inevitability of sin, and consequent limita‑
tion on his anger. The short concluding exhortation to virtue
refers to the pure soul as a pearl, a comparison made inter‑
mittently throughout the poem, and in other poems of the
group.

The Destruction of Sodom and Gomorrah (ll. 556–1048). This
middle part of the poem begins with a linking homily, in
which a description of God's sorrow for bringing about the
Flood leads into further expressions of horror at the lechery
which brings down divine vengeance, and an indication of
the next subject. The organization of the story of the Destruc‑
tion, like that of Belshazzar's Feast in the last part of the
poem, is much more complex than that of the story of the
Flood. There are two longish introductory sections, the one
containing God's promises to Abraham, that his seed will
inherit the earth and that he himself will have an heir, and
the other recording Abraham's plea to God to spare his
kinsman Lot. Doctrinally they reassure the reader of God's
continuous care for mankind, even though another divine
action of immense and terrifying destruction is being pre‑
pared; and they also show covenanted and virtuous man, in
the person of Abraham and, in a smaller role, of Lot, work‑
ing within the scheme of God's will to help shape and fulfil
divine aims. Before the doom erupts in the Dead Sea cities
there are two sacramental feasts, one prepared by Abraham
for the 'three men', one of whom appears to be God, and the
other prepared by Lot for the 'two angels'. Both are reflec‑
tions, foretokens, of the Marriage Feast, and of that heavenly
'feast where all the faithful feed in fine solemnity' ('St
Erkenwald', l. 336): they stand in contrast to the godless
gourmandizing and tippling of Belshazzar's Feast in the last
part of the poem. At the meals at the homes of Abraham and
Lot the occluded vision of the two women, Sarah and Lot's

wife, figures prominently. Priestly anti-feminism may in part account for this, but if so, the poet's omission in not presenting to us Noah's wife as well is extraordinary. The certain explanation is that men consecrated to God must be tested and seen to stand the test; and Sarah and Lot's wife, both disloyal to God, did do things the withstanding of which brought credit on their spouses, while the comic and discreditable traditions concerning Noah – his drunkenness, his scolding wife – do nothing to illuminate the concept of Noah the man of God. With equal structural decorum the poet omits the episode in which his two daughters lie with the drunken Lot, in order, as they think, to preserve the seed of the race.

The Destruction itself, like the Flood, prefigures Judgement Day, when the blessed ascend to eternal life, and the sinners go down into hell. The cataclysm seen from far off by Abraham, and the subsequently *Dead* Sea described by the poet, are types of hell.

The great homily on Cleanness, linking the Destruction of Sodom and Gomorrah with Belshazzar's Feast, opens with interpretative advice to the reader:

> All these are tokens and types to turn over in the mind.
>
> (1049)

But the material he now presents is the central matter of his religion, of which other things and events may be 'tokens and types'.

Accordingly, there is an abrupt change of style. After the grim narration of events in the valley of the Dead Sea, the homily strikes as with the sudden force of musical mollification after prolonged *fortissimo*. The poet writes with the impassioned lyricism of mystical love. He brings the techniques of courtly love poetry into play with new subject-matter drawn from popular traditions about the adoration of the Virgin and Christ, to make his audience aspire to holy cleanness. The imagery is all of perfection – rose scent, musical harmony, pearls flawless and polished; a perfection which is incorruptible, as is shown when it makes contact with diseased nature. Christ's healing power chimes with his courtesy to summon yearning man. As the poet warns against allowing the pearl–soul to lose its brightness shut up in a box, the lyric mood slips from him, and almost without noticing it, we are back with the Old Testament thunderer fulminating about the vengeance of God. From neglected jewellery it is a short transition to misused holy utensils, the subject of the last, and longest, *exemplum*.

Belshazzar's Feast (ll. 1157–1812). The drowning of the generation of Noah for both impurity and disloyalty had as prelude the suffering, but not destruction, of Lucifer and Adam for disloyalty alone. The destruction of Sodom and Gomorrah for impurity and disloyalty had as prelude the punishment of Lot's wife and the exposure of Sarah, both for disloyalty. Similarly, the slaughter of Belshazzar and his supporters for disloyalty and impurity has as supporting examples the defeat and captivity of Zedekiah, and the madness of Nebuchadnezzar, both for disloyalty alone. But the preparation for catastrophe is lengthy and complicated in this last section: the story of Nebuchadnezzar's madness is told by Daniel, after the Writing on the Wall has appeared (ll. 1641–1708), quite separately from the account of Nebuchadnezzar's conquest of Jerusalem, which comes at the beginning of the section. There is a special reason for the telling of this long tale about the sack of Jerusalem and the carrying of the Temple ornaments and vessels to Babylon. This is to attach such holiness to the great candlestick (the Menorah) and the other temple utensils that the reader will take misuse of them, when the time comes, as greater 'uncleanness' than the un/natural seed/squandering of the generation of Noah or the homosexual lusts of the men of Sodom and Gomorrah. Charles Moorman,[4] citing Fr Edwin Cuffe, suggests that the consecrated Temple vessels may be anagogies for conse/crated souls. If this is so, then Belshazzar commits the crime of forcing the consecrated to become backsliders; and throughout the poem God punishes backsliders more severely than other sinners. So Belshazzar is not only un/clean and disloyal in himself, but the powerful cause of un/cleanness and disloyalty in others. Zedekiah's sin was disloyalty,

> Embracing abominations and bowing to idols (1173)

and Nebuchadnezzar's was pride. Both kings were back/sliders, but into disloyalty only, not uncleanness.

The Holy of Holies, in the Temple, is an anagogy for heaven. When Nebuzardan brings the ornaments and ves/sels to Babylon, Nebuchadnezzar recognizes not merely their intrinsic value, but

> Seizing them solemnly, he spoke praise to the Sovereign
> Who was high lord of all, Israel's God. (1313–14)

Bestowing them 'royally and with reverence', he preserves their holy potential, and so has grace in God's eyes, until his pride brings his downfall. Even that pride, however, is purged by his penance in the wilderness. It is as if God never forgot that he had used Nebuchadnezzar initially as his instrument of vengeance upon Zedekiah.

As for the feast which Belshazzar gave, its symbolic values must be stated. The city in which it occurred has

---

4. *The Pearl/Poet* (Twayne, 1968), p. 81.

seven rivers, and each of the four sides of the palace enclosure was seven miles long; seven being the number associated with earthly things, in contrast to the twelves of the New Jerusalem, as given in Revelation xxi and celebrated by the poet in 'Pearl'. Then, incidental proof that this is no holy feast comes with the information that only nobles are bidden to the feast. In the Parable of the Marriage Feast all people of all classes were bidden, though indeed the poet in his account does seat the guests in order of rank. The beauty of the precious objects is described with an intensity which clearly expresses the poet's longing for God; the Menorah stands for the light of heaven, and when it illuminates the Writing on the Wall God's ultimate power is manifest:

> In that princely palace, on a plain wall,
> Close by where the candelabrum most clearly shone,
> There appeared a spirit hand with pen between fingers.
>
> (1531–3)

Belshazzar's queen, who stayed in 'her quarters above' during the idolatrous banqueting, tropologically represents resistance to temptation: as the instrument by means of which God's representative, Daniel, is brought into action, she naturally personifies courtly beauty, and observes the exact etiquette of courtesy, which we have already come to see as a part of cleanness:

> The lady, to lessen the loss of her lord,
> Glided down graciously to go to the King.
>
> On the cold stone kneeling, she sank, and spoke to him
> Words of wisdom, in a worshipful manner.   (1589–92)

The poet's final focus on Daniel and Belshazzar enables him to make his last point illustrate his first statement of all. The poem began with a description of true and false priests (ll. 5–16), and ends with the exaltation of a true priest who knows the mind of God, and the destruction and damnation of a false idol-worshipper who desecrated God's utensils. On every count Belshazzar exemplifies the evil against which the poet warns, for not only is he perversely licentious and disloyal to God, but he is also a backslider, because his father Nebuchadnezzar had brought him up to honour God. And having disposed of Belshazzar the poet has no need of more than the slightest formal conclusion and blessing.

The poet's use of patristic exegesis had to be explained in order for his poetic gifts, and especially his power of construction, to be appreciated. And to these gifts I now turn, although readers of his better-known poems, chief of which is 'Sir Gawain and the Green Knight', will recognize them, freshly expressed through both familiar and strange excellences, as they read 'Cleanness'.

The fascination for many is the poet's quality, which is like no other poet's in its combination of narrative economy, descriptive power, eloquent persuasion, and grim irony. For example, the last thirty-three lines of the poem cover an immense range of expression, from a description of a grisly death to a final blessing which with remarkable brevity restates the moral aim of the poem. They even include one of the poet's savage jokes. Belshazzar would be

> most probably deprived of pleasures above, too –
> His looking on our lovely Lord would be long deferred!
>
> (1803–4)

Such jokes always seem to be at the expense of the victims of the action being described. Even the host of the Parable of the Marriage Feast, who after all stands for God, witheringly scorns the man in rags. And the plight of the remnant of the population of Jerusalem, when Nebuzardan at last bursts through the battlements, is described without pity; in fact, the poet has a great grim joke at the expense of both besiegers and besieged;

> What! a tiny triumph, for the troops were away,
> The good ones all gone with the governor of the city.
> And the men who remained were so miserably starved,
> One woman would have been worth the most warrior-like
> four.   (1241-4)

He also pokes more legitimate fun at the Chaldean magicians who cannot read the Writing on the Wall:

> They looked at the letters and were enlightened no more
> Than if they'd looked at the leather of my left boot.
>   (1581-2)

That kind of savage humour is found in Icelandic saga – characters like Skarpheddin son of Njal revel in it – and it goes quaintly with the fastidious sense of courtesy possessed by the poet, which is not at all like the stark and primitive decorum which is its equivalent in saga. The courtesy of 'Cleanness' is a medieval quality, compounded of Christian good manners and the etiquette of Romance *courts*, from which the word derives. All his hosts except the drivelling Belshazzar show exquisite and delicate decorum when they entertain. The host of the parable walks from table to table welcoming and cheering his human guests, and Abraham and Lot show the higher and therefore holy courtesy of recognizing that their guests are divine, and behave accordingly.

This holy courtesy operates like a moving ceremony, in which every action, every word, has the force of ritual. But the exercise of hospitality depends on ritual anyway, and the purest kind of courtesy needs no such prop. We shall find it working at times of crisis, when the man has nothing to support him except his spirit. Abraham shows it when pleading with God for the life of his kinsman Lot, as he moves with extraordinary gentleness and persistence against the divine will, to modify it (ll. 713–80). The crowning expression of it is to let God walk away, having promised to spare Sodom if ten good men are found there, and then to call out a reminder that Lot lived there – a logical and harmoniously pathetic addition to the account in Genesis xviii. And Lot shows the same courtesy in an even less promising situation, when he goes out to temporize with the homosexual rioters at his gate and, as he thinks, to protect his holy guests from them.

> What! he feared not the fury of those filthy knaves,
> But passed through the portal to the peril that awaited . . .
> Hoping to lessen their lechery by his lofty courtesy.
>
> (855–6, 860)

Developing a hint from the Bible, the poet manages Lot's speech, in which he offers his daughters to the men in his attempt to protect the honour of his visitors, with quite remarkable tact. It is a situation distasteful to any age but a primitive one in which female children are regarded as mere chattels, and is justifiable only on the same terms as those upon which one accepts the story of Abraham and Isaac. But Lot somehow retains his medieval courtesy:

> You are jolly gentlemen indeed, but your japes are unseemly.
> Let me teach you a trick more temptingly natural. (864–5)

Through Lot, the poet somehow enters the thought-world of the rioters, but even so manages to put into his mouth the key-word 'natural', to remind the reader of the kind of sexual activity God approves.

The word 'natural', however, does not take us very far, in the light of modern anthropological and psychological investigation. We are still discovering. Broadly speaking, the medieval schoolmen did not wish to discover, and so found that their own formulation, 'natural', gave them convenient limits within which to confine their speculations and moral approval. But, being 'natural' themselves, they often found it hard to confine their emotions when they speculated upon human love in all its manifestations, and hard to accommodate their ascetic thought and way of life to it. And so it was with the poet of 'Cleanness', whose whole scheme of thought appears to be dominated by a fascinated horror of sex, which he expresses in two ways. The moral condemnation, such as

> Yet in fleshly deeds they invented filthy practices,
> Having new and unnatural knowledge of each other,
>
> (265-6)

is often followed by visual explicitness, like

> So foul were their fleshly doings that fiends, observing
> Of this race how rare and ravishing were the daughters,
> Fell to fornicating with them, in the fashion of humans.
>
> (269-71)

Similarly, he describes the sinners of Sodom:

> They have learnt of a lust that I little like,
> Having found the filthiest of fleshly perversions.
> Each male takes as mate a man like himself,
> And they couple carnally, clasped as man and woman.
>
> (693-6)

The charge should not be pressed too hard, but since, in the whole work of this poet, there is no instance of licit love between a specific man and woman, nor of sexual love having a place in any of his themes except as an adjunct of other qualities, it has to be said that his emphasis on sexual uncleanness places him among the obsessives of the medieval Church, who saw love narrowly, and overrated the seriousness of sin in sexual matters.

In his main argument, that uncleanness is the worst of all sins and most hated by God, our author had run counter to the teaching of all medieval theology, which declared Pride to be the chief of the Seven Deadly Sins, and relegated Lechery to the end of the list

notes Mabel Day, apparently thinking, erroneously, that the placing of the sins in the list implied grading in moral obloquy.[5] She instances the fact that *The Book of the Knight of La Tour Landry*, which was written in 1373 for the instruction of the knight's daughters in preparation for marriage, has twenty-eight chapters on Uncleanness, and only five on Pride. But I think that she and Gollancz, who establish beyond reasonable doubt that the poet had read the good knight's work, make the wrong point. The important thing is that the poet chose his theme for his own reasons, and in writing upon it, would, in the spirit of normal medieval eclecticism, make use of anything he could find already written upon it.

This brings us to the quite extraordinary twelve lines the poet puts into the mouth of God, in which he celebrates ideal human love nostalgically, as part of his lament for the vices of Sodom and Gomorrah. He is facing, and asking his readers to face, the perennial problem of resolving the doctrinal conflict between the spirit and the flesh. The forbear of Christianity, Judaism, seems on the whole to have made better sense of the deed of kind than the younger and more ascetic religion, but in the latter it yet had its allotted place – often awarded somewhat grudgingly by theologians of a Pauline disposition. The passage goes far beyond what is usual in religious writing and is successful, beyond dreams of what

5. Gollancz, *Cleanness* (EETS, Oxford, 1921), vol. 2, p. 76.

might be thought possible in that mode, in harmonizing the
ethos of courtly love with that of Christianity. Gollancz
notes[6] that marriage is praised in *The Book of the Knight of La
Tour Landry*, which, however, is not concerned with Christian doctrine. Here are God's words:

> I made them natural means, which I communicated secretly,
> And held most holy in my ordinance for humans,
> A manner of mating of marvellous sweetness.
> In my brain was born the embrace of lovers:
>
> The modes of love I made for man's utmost delight,
> That when two true ones are attached to each other,
> Between the man and his mate is such mutual joy
> That the purity of Paradise could prove little better;
>
> Provided each to each is honourably joined
> By a still secret voice, unstirred by sight,
> With the love-flame leaping, lashed so hot
> That all the evils on earth could not quench it.
>
> (697–708)

Everything turns, as the discerning reader will observe, on
the meaning of that word 'true'. To the devotees of courtly
love it referred only to the depth, power and constancy of
passion, irrespective of the social and religious law; so that it
could certainly cover adulterous love, as in that most famous
and fatal of medieval love-affairs, between Tristan and Isolde.
But 'true' is a key-word of the poem, and 'truth to God'
(the poet's word is *trawpe*) means the exact following of his
law in a spirit of generous and consenting loyalty (of which,
paradoxically, Lot's offering of his virgin daughters to the
lustful homosexuals is probably the finest example in the
poem). This 'truth' the poet wants to dominate every aspect
of man's life; accordingly his whole religious faith goes into

6. op. cit., vol. I, p. xiv.

his delineation of the ideal God-created relationship between man and woman. So he has no difficulty in absorbing into his Christian scheme elements of the ideal of courtly love which derive ultimately from the classical heritage of the Middle Ages, fundamentally pagan though they may be. He simply presents them, in their perfect form, as able to ward off 'all the evils on earth', and so gives them a transcendental moral quality. This may well be nearer to the truth (using the word in its modern sense) than any attitude based on a conception of the fundamental antipathy in the soul between the flesh and the spirit; and the view of the poet is more acceptable in its explicitness than, for example, the expressed views of those two great English poets and Christian apolo-gists for marriage, Spenser and Milton. After these twelve lines the account of Adam and Eve mating in Book 4 of *Paradise Lost* reads like an embarrassed and distasteful accommodation with what is 'natural'. But the poet's idealization and compartmentalization of love are part of his wider yearning for God, and his attitude has to be seen in the context of his conception of the wrath of God, which figures so prominently in the poem.

It seems that, of the three parts of the soul as conceived by scholastic philosophy, the rational, the irascible and the con-cupiscent, the God of the poem partakes of the first two, and these two are at conflict within him, as they often are in humans, as he experiences the desire for vengeance against successive evil-doers in the poem. An ancient Eastern Christian theory of the nature of God, which seems to me to throw light on this problem, divides it into *essence* and *energy*. His essence is to be rational, which, applied to these circumstances, means that he will exercise justice tempered with mercy. But his energy, his vital power to act, suffuses his essence with such righteous indignation that vindictiveness threatens him. God is thus a paradigm of a society threatened by disruptive internal forces; but with this difference, that, unlike Man, he is not fallen, so that neither his rational and irascible parts nor his fundamental essence and energy can be corrupted into wrong thought or action. So the measure of whatever emotional conflict we see in him is simply a measure of the degree of sinfulness in Man. In the judgements of God, by whatever means they are determined, the poet profoundly concurs. For him the wrath of God is an instrument which makes the pursuit of perfection possible, because it destroys evil; and he is, in this poem, especially interested in the wrath of God when it punishes lechery.

The portrayal of the great manifestations of God's wrath constitutes one of the poem's main attractions; but in admiring the sheer splendour and violence, the equal command of panorama and significant detail – which is exercised as if the poet possessed a kind of zoom lens which enables him to take in a flooding planet in one half-second, and two despairing lovers clinging together in the next – the reader must never forget his constancy of homiletic purpose, and his easy and unobtrusive power to fill his scenes with suggestive and relevant symbols. Readers who remember with pleasure Sir Gawain's trials at the hands of hard Nature and the supernatural,[7] or Jonah's experiences in the Mediterranean storm and within the belly of the whale[8] (the one a type of God's wrath, the other of hell), will, I think, be even more excited by the accounts of destruction in 'Cleanness'.

The first of these, describing the casting out of the rebel angels from heaven, gives a foretaste of the more tremendous

7. e. g. Brian Stone (trans.,) *Sir Gawain and the Green Knight* (Penguin, 2nd edn, 1974), pp. 48, 98–104.

8. Brian Stone (trans.), *Medieval English Verse* (Penguin, 1964), pp. 124–9.

descriptions of the Flood and the Destruction of Sodom and Gomorrah: in twenty-eight lines the event and its theological analysis are completed, with an almost nonchalant display of the poet's finest and most characteristic qualities. Instantaneity of violent effect and exactness of homiletic focus come strictly together: when Lucifer affirms that he will 'be like the Lord who laid out the firmament', then

> The very moment he averred it, vengeance fell upon him;
> The Deity sternly doomed him, and drove him to the abyss,
> With measure in his majesty, his mercy held in balance.
>
> (213–15)

Simile, concrete and even domestic in origin, justly enriches his description:

> Black fiends falling from the firmament on high,
> Swirling at the first stroke like snow in a storm,
> Hurled into hell-hole like a hive swarming . . .
>
> But like strained meal which smokes most in a small sieve,
> That horrid shower hurtling from heaven to hell
> Hung all round the earth, everywhere the same.
>
> (221–3, 226–8)

The second great destruction of the poem brings humans into the grasp of God; distant devils tumbling somehow do not touch us, but when we read that

> Every mother with infant ran out of her house,
> Hurried to the high places, the highest there were,
>
> (378–9)

and that

> The lover and his lady looked their last farewell,
> Ending everything for all time, for ever parting,
>
> (401–2)

we acknowledge that we are in the hands of a master of pathos, and suffer with the people described; even though we know that they were responsible for turning what God made into more of a hell than a paradise. 'Mother with infant' and 'the lover and his lady' were among the giants who

> so jeopardized the gentle creation
> That God the great maker began to be angry.   (279-80)

The account of the deluge gathers force by a series of fluxes; several times it seems that everything has in fact been submerged – human beings, animals, high land, and mountains. But each time the description returns to a slightly lower level, and a new phase of watery invasion, a freshly harrowing account of the panic and pleading of the afflicted as they strive to avoid drowning, reinforce what has gone before. And at the last, when flux after gigantic flux has absolutely soaked the mind, it is left with that tiny little ark, aloft on the heaving watery surface of a drowned planet, the highest mountains of which are fifteen cubits below the keel; yardsticks of the almost immeasurable gulfs of water below. There is a dizzy sense of the height at which the ark is floating, and of its utter helplessness, in

The ark was thrown high on the heaving currents,
Rolled close to the clouds over countries unknown.
It weltered on the wild waters, went where it would,
Drove above the depths, in danger as it seemed . . .

It could float only forwards as the fell winds blew,
Or waver with the water, or be washed back.
Often it rolled around, often reared on end;
Hard things would have happened, had the helmsman not been
    God.   (413-16, 421-4)

That throw-away doctrinal nudge about God the helmsman is timed to coincide with the poet's detaching from the scene to review the effects of the Flood, before he goes on to describe the ebbing. He follows the rhythm of the Biblical account, providing idyllic calm for the moment of the successful dove's return; and he invests the re-possession of the earth by man and beast with an ebullient bursting forth of life appropriate to each species, ending with the major-key coda of

> Every beast hurried off to his own habitat,
> And the four men remaining were masters of the world.
>
> (539-40)

The third destruction of the poem is more localized and intense than the two preceding. Lucifer's legions were driven by

> That horrid shower hurtling from heaven to earth   (227)

and the Flood came because 'the abyss burst forth' accompanied by forty days of rain. But actual hell, complete with its hounds, erupts at Sodom and Gomorrah, and sucks the cities into itself to the accompaniment of a violent storm in heaven. The cleft of the Dead Sea no doubt preserves a terrifying racial memory of the earthquake and its accompanying storm; to this day it is frightening to look down into it from the hills to the west. Mamre is near the highest point (3,346 feet above sea level) between Jerusalem and Hebron; from this point one can see the blue of the not-so-distant Mediterranean on one side, and on the other, the blue of the Dead Sea, so ominously lower (1,286 feet below sea level) than the oceans of the world, and often partly hazy, as if hell were gently simmering just below. From such a height to such a depth Abraham looked in grief when God had done his work (ll. 1001-8).

To that lowest point on the surface of the earth attention is directed long before there is any talk of destruction. When God and his two angels say good-bye to Abraham after their entertainment,

> Then rapidly they rose, making ready to go,
> And in a group together, they gazed towards Sodom.
>
> (671-2)

An ominous suspense is gradually built up as divine retribution is planned, and humans react in emotion. The feelings of Lucifer and Noah were not mentioned, although Noah was pretty brisk in his efforts to have the ark built and loaded on time; but Abraham grieves both for his kinsman Lot and for humanity when the destruction of Sodom is in prospect, and as time runs out in the dawn Lot is terrified, doubting his power and his deserving to escape the wrath of God. The description of the four fleeing,

> Their flesh full of fear as they fled on together,
> At the double, in dread, never daring to look back,
>
> (975-6)

reminds me of panicking mobs, of which I have been a member, running stunned from big explosions. The Destruction itself is full of fire, uproar and stink (all recognized attributes of hell), and its annihilation of the natural scene is presented, as was the Fall of the Angels, by means of a vivid domestic simile:

> Then crags and cliffs were cloven in shreds
> Like loose leaves of a book that flutter about. (955-6)

It is a localized and intense destruction indeed, but it lacks the degrading sense of personal violation with which the poet invests his final destruction, the slaughter of Belshazzar. As in all his poems, he achieves progression in a variety of ways, and the measure of horror in the last destruction he describes is the extent to which actual bodies are torn and mutilated. Whole bodies were drowned in the Flood, whole bodies sank shrieking into hell at Sodom; we were not given the smell of burning flesh or the disintegration of limbs from bodies as hell-hounds snapped and tore. But the prelude, the antetype, of the destruction of Belshazzar forces upon us hideous atrocity in punishment for hideous crime. Nebuchadnezzar, after defeating the forces which made a sortie from besieged Jerusalem,

> ... slew each king's son in the sight of his father,
> With great grimness gouged out his eyes. (1221–2)

And the forces of Nebuzardan, when at last they break into the city,

> Priests and prelates they pressed to death,
> And the wombs of wives and wenches they cut open
> So that their bowels bubbled about in the ditches;
>
> (1250–52)

and

> Held the priests by the hair and hacked off their heads,
> Did deacons to death, struck down the clerks,
> And all the maidens of the minster they murdered atrociously
> In the swath of the swords that destroyed them all. (1265–8)

In the last punishment mentioned in the poem

> Belshazzar was battered to death in his bed,
> His blood and his brains blending with the sheets.
> Then the king was caught up in his curtain by the heels,
> Dragged forth by the feet and foully abused –
> He who that day had so daringly drunk from the vessels.
>
> (1787–91)

So the fate of the generation of Noah is the most cosmically frightening; that of Sodom and Gomorrah the most locally horrifying and intimate to man's emotions; and that of Belshazzar and his antetypes the most intestinally atrocious and the most destitute of all human feeling. 'Enough! And too much.'

The vividness and concentration which can sicken when the subject is vengeance, delight when it is beauty or mysterious symbol. The ornamentation of the Temple vessels, the pomp of Belshazzar's Feast, and the Dead Sea as a type of hell after the Destruction of Sodom and Gomorrah, Gollancz (pp. 26–8) has shown probably to be derived from Mandeville's *Travels*; but the organization of the descriptions, the symbolic interpretations he places on the subjects, and above all the bold alliterative flow of the verse, belong to the poet alone.

Any poet who bases a long work on the Bible, or indeed any other work of literature, must continually draw inspiration from his original. The quality of 'Cleanness' is to seem like the Bible in the weight of its argument and description, and yet to be something quite itself. R. J. Menner notes that three fifths of the lines of the poem have their source in the Latin of the Vulgate, but whether this refers only to subject matter, or to verbal meaning, he does not state. The best way to gauge the poet's powers of selection and development is to follow the source story in the Bible while reading the poem; the main references are given in the footnotes.

The final impression left by this complex and highly organized Bible epic is of a curiously inharmonious vision; inharmonious because the dark and the light in it do not seem to be properly balanced. The stated intention of the poet is to 'acclaim Cleanness in becoming style', but in fact his overwhelming achievement is to dispraise uncleanness, which he does so energetically, so unremittingly, that he forgets the balancing need, which the reader feels emotionally, to maintain to the end the reality of the compensating beatific vision which is the reward for cleanness. Although it must be understood that the poet is following accepted preaching practice in recommending a virtue by condemning its opposite, yet it is worth noting that nowhere else in his work does he leave the reader suffused with such an agonized sense of the evil in man, a belief that

> The mind of man is inclined mostly to evil, (518)

In 'Patience' and 'Pearl' the end is reconciliation, balance, understanding of the self after hard test and suffering; qualities expressed continuously in the much more complex 'Sir Gawain and the Green Knight', in which the poet maintains a penetrating detachment throughout. In 'Cleanness' the beatific vision, like the wonderful praise of true love, is confined in a corner of the poet's artefact, while his revulsion from the evil in man has licence to rampage, horsed by the wrath of God. Yet belief in the essential cleanness of the soul is there, though muted. 'Unlawful lechery which lays waste the self' (l. 579) is somehow an outside force come to corrupt 'the gentle creation' (l. 279), like those 'immoderate monsters' (l. 273), and it is possible for the self to keep clean. To Noah and his family, to Abraham, to Belshazzar's queen and to Daniel, an angel might justly have said, as he did to Lot: 'You're strangely your*self* still, though sin surrounds you' (l. 923).

The poet finds, and recommends the reader to find, refuge from rampaging leachery in sacrament with God, of which the priest, with his ceremonies and utensils, is the instrument. This man, who paces to God's altar, and handles God's body in holy communion (l. 11), is there by powerful surro-

gate at every stage in the poem at which God's covenant with
man is re-affirmed, whether before or after, or even during,
one of the great destructions. His power is to conduct courteous ceremonies, at which the word of God is heard and
interpreted for the benefit of Man. He is there when the Flood
subsides, as Noah who

> raised up an altar and hallowed it duly,
> And set on it a sacrifice of every sort of creature.
> That was comely and clean – God cares for nothing else:
> (506–8)

and heard the promise of God never again to destroy the
whole of creation. He is there as Abraham, feasting the God
who is to promise his seed a mighty inheritance; he is there as
Lot, presiding over the sacramental meal which ensures his
survival and is prelude to the destruction of the cities of the
sodomites. And he is there in the spirit of the dead Solomon,
whose piety and industry made the incomparably clean
vessels of the Temple, so impregnating them with pure
essence that they give out testimony even when carried off to
Babylon, and attract the writing hand of God to warn of the
vengeance to come. And he is there lastly in Daniel, to tell
the last story of God's vengeance and forgiveness, in the case
of Nebuchadnezzar; and to use that story to demonstrate
that it is impossible for Belshazzar to be redeemed. From the
ensuing scene of slaughter he emerges as himself, to give his
final warning, and his final blessing. They come from a man
who knows that humanity is imperfectible, and whose concern with sexual licence has led him to compose, almost as a
refuge from what he finds it hard to bear, a momentous
dream of the wrath of God.

CLEANNESS

Prologue
The Parable of the Marriage Feast

He who would acclaim Cleanness in becoming style,
And rehearse all the honours she asks as of right,
May find fair forms to further his art:
To utter the opposite would be hard and troublesome.[1]

For he who made all is angry to a marvel
With votaries who follow him with defiled spirits.
Consider the sacred calling of those who sing and read
And approach his presence, priests as we call them:

Attached to him in truth, to his temple they go;
Properly and piously they pace to his altar
And handle his own body in holy communion.
If Cleanness encompass them, how incomparable their reward!

But if their faith is false and failing in courtesy,
Their outsides all honour, their insides corrupted,
They are sinful themselves and sullied altogether,
Hating God and his good rites, goading him to anger.[2]

So clean in his court is that king who rules all,
So upright a householder, so honourably served

1. 'To utter the opposite', i.e. to dispraise cleanness.
2. This is the only attack on corrupt churchmen in the whole
work of the 'Pearl' poet.

77

By angels of utter purity without and within,
Beautifully bright, in brilliant mantles,[3]

That it would seem most strange, stretching improbability,
If he did not disdain and put down evil.
Christ said it himself in a sermon once,
Exalting eight beatitudes and their high rewards.[4]

One remains in my mind as Matthew records it,
Clearly describing Cleanness in these terms:
Fair shall befall the fully pure in heart:
They shall look on Our Lord in blithe humility.

He says besides, that sight shall never be seen
By any who have uncleanness anywhere about them.
For he who has flung foulness far from his heart
Cannot bear a body that is blemished near him.

So hasten not to heaven in odious rags,
Nor in a hireling's hood, with hands unwashed;
For what holder of high honour, what earthly noble,
Would approve a rascal arriving wretchedly dressed,

When he himself on the high seat was solemnly attended,
Above dukes on the dais, with delicacies served?
For a lout to leap in and slouch to the table,
His trashy breeks tattered, leggings torn at the knee,

3. The raiment of angels symbolizes their purity of spirit.
4. It was a standard procedure for homiletic writers to focus on
the Beatitudes in their introductions. The poet details them at the
beginning of 'Patience'.

His tabard torn too, his toes sticking out![5]
For any or all of these, they'd haul him outside
With abundant rebukes, and blows perhaps.
Hurl him to the hall door, heave him hard out of it,

And tell him tersely to return no more
On pain of imprisonment and being put in the stocks.
Thus shall he be shamed for his shabby clothing,
Though he attempted no trespass by tongue or by touch.

If his welcome by a worldly prince so warned him off,
The high king of heaven would be harder on him still.
Remember the wealthy man in Matthew's gospel,[6]
Who made a mighty banquet for the marriage of his heir,

And then sent his servants to assemble guests,
Inviting them to the feast in their finest attire:
'My bulls and my boars have been baited and killed,[7]
And my finely fed fowls fattened for slaughter,

'My pen-fed poultry, my partridges too,
Swans and storks: these with sides of wild boar
Are all broiled and roasted and ready to eat.
Come to my court, quickly before it cools!'

When they heard of the host's hospitable summons,
All declined with excuses of whatever colour they could
   think of.

   5. The tabard was a sleeveless peasant's shirt, which developed
later into a knight's surcoat.
   6. Matthew xxii, 1–14, but the poet does not include vv. 6–7 in
his paraphrase.
   7. Animals might be baited by dogs before being slaughtered,
to improve the taste of the meat. (See Cawley and Anderson, op.
cit., p. 53.)

One had purchased a place, upon his faith, he said,
'And I must go at great speed to gaze on the estate.'

Another said, 'No' and announced his reason:
'My heart was set on oxen, and now I've a pair;
My bondsmen have bought them, and I'm bound to go
To see them pull the plough: I'm pledged to do it.'

'And I've wedded a wife,' were the words of a third,
'Excuse me from your court, I cannot be present.'
So protesting and temporizing, they turned away one and all,
Not entering the house, though earnestly entreated.

This was little to the liking of the lord of those people:
Indignant at their doings, in deep dudgeon he said,
'They seek their own sorrow in forsaking me thus;
Their badness is more blameworthy than blind Gentile sin. [8]

'So go forth, my good men, to the great thoroughfares,
Seek through the city, search all its streets.
Wayfaring folk on foot and on horseback,
Both mighty and meek, whether men or maidens,

'Call on them courteously to come to my banquet,
And guide them graciously to my great hall like nobles,
So that my palace shall be plentifully packed with people.
Dishonour to those others! I abhor their unworthiness.'

8. 'Gentile' is a synonym for 'heathen' in middle English.
Throughout, the poet affirms that God is harder on backsliders
than on those who never knew grace.

Then away they went, those who watched over the region,
And brought in bachelors met on the border hills,
Squires who swiftly spurred after on their steeds,
And many folk on foot, both free and bond.

When they came to the court, they were courteously en-
    treated,
Escorted by the steward, who stationed them in hall,
And made them sit by the marshal in mannerly style,
Ranged in right order as their rank determined.

The servants said to their sovereign then,
'Lo! Lord, by your leave, at your liege command,
We have brought as you bade us, by your order,
Many alien men, yet there's much room for more.'

The lord replied to his liegemen, 'Look everywhere,
Farther afield, and fetch more guests.
Search the gorsy heaths and groves and gather in
All folk that you find there, fetch them hither.

'Whether fierce or feeble, don't fail to bring them.
Whether they're hale, or halt, or have only one eye,
Or are even eyeless and hobbling helplessly,
They shall cram the corners of my castle to overflowing.

'For certainly these same men who sent their excuses,
Spurning what I proffered at this present time,
Shall never savour my supper, sitting in my hall,
Nor swallow one sip of my soup, though they suffer death.'

He spoke, and his servants sallied forth
To fulfil faithfully his firm command;
And they packed the palace with people of all kinds,
Not sons of a single mother, sired by one father.

Whether less or more worthy, they were well bestowed,
Those in brightest habiliments, the best, first,
And those held in most honour at the high dais;
Then along the length of the table, those of lower degree.

And always the status of each sitter could be seen from his
    clothes.[9]
So by this marshalling at the meal all men were honoured,
The renown of the noblest by no means neglected,
And the simplest, just the same, served in full

With meat and fine minstrelsy and many an honour,
And no lack of the delights a lord should provide;
And the good wine going round, gaiety prevailed,
With each man at ease with the other guests.

The Punishment of the Man without
a Wedding Garment

Now in the middle of the meal the master resolved
To see those sitting assembled there,
And happily honour both the high and the low,
Cherishing them with his cheer, re-charging their joy.

So he quit his own quarters, came into the wide hall
To the best on the bench and bade them be merry,
Speaking words of welcome; then walked farther down
From table to table, gaily talking all the time.[10]

9. The feudal variety of Christianity shows in this deference to
rank at the Marriage Feast, which stands for the souls' community
with God; there is no mention of the status of the guests in Matthew. But in 'Pearl' the poet asserts the absolute equality of saved
souls in heaven enjoined by the Parable of the Vineyard.

10. This is a description of standard courtly etiquette for the host.

But as he went over the floor his eye fell on
One hardly habited for a holiday occasion,
A thrall in the thick of the throng in rags,
Not in festival finery, but filthy with toil,

A man not dressed for dealing with decent men.
The high lord was angry, and aimed to punish him.
With a louring look, the lord said, 'Tell me,
My friend, how you find yourself here so foully clad?

'The habit you're in does the holy day no honour.
It wasn't for a wedding that you wore that garb!
How so hardy as to enter this house unluckily
In so tattered a turn-out, all torn at the sides?

'A disgraceful garment, you ungodly man!
You price me and my palace poorly and meanly,
Pressing your approach to my presence like this.
Do you suppose I'm a peasant who'll praise your mantle?'[11]

The fellow was confounded by these furious words
And hung down his head, his eyes on the ground:[12]
His spirit was so paralysed as he expected a blow
That there wasn't a word he could whisper with sense.

Then the lord let fly in his loudest voice
To his team of torturers. 'Take him,' he ordered,
'Bind at his back both his hands,
And fix harsh fetters to his feet at once!

11. The poet uses the word *erigaut*, which was a fashionable
short upper garment; so the irony is intentional.
12. This is the traditional posture of Shame.

'Set him straight in the stocks, then sternly lock him
Deep in my dungeon, the dwelling of grief,
Where weeping and wailing with woeful gnashing
Of teeth shall teach him to attire himself properly.'

Christ by this account likens the kingdom of heaven
To a marvellous meal to which many are invited.
For all who in holy water were ever baptized
Are bid fairly to the feast, both the defiled and the good.

But watch, if you will, that you wear clean clothes
To honour the holy day, lest harm come to you
When you approach that Prince of precious lineage –
He hates not even hell more hotly than the unclean.

Then what sort of wear should you swathe yourself in
To show by its shimmering a shining excellence?
Without doubt the deeds you have done are your clothes,
Which are lined with the longings that lie in your heart;

If they are found to be fair and fresh in your life,
And finely fashioned to fit at feet and hands,
And all your other parts are habited immaculately,
You may see your Saviour and his seat of majesty.

Profuse are the faults which may forfeit man's bliss
And the sight of his Sovereign: sloth is one;
Boasting and bragging, and bulging pride,
Thrust man most thoroughly down the throat of the Devil.[13]

13. In Church and manuscript paintings, and on the medieval
stage, Hell-mouth was terrifyingly represented as the maw of a
monster.

Covetousness, cunning and crooked dealing,[14]
Forswearing, manslaughter, excessive drinking,
Stealing and squabbling, expose him to harm.
Burglary, bawdry, bandying lies,

Leaving widows out of wills, making away with dowries,
Undermining marriages, maintaining malefactors,
Treason and treachery and tyranny as well,
Defaming falsely, fraudulent law-making –

Indeed man may miss that much-praised bliss
For such sins as these; suffer in agony,
And never come to the court of the Creator at the last,
Or behold him with his eyes, for such heinous practices.

I

God's Vengeance on Lucifer, and on Adam

Though I have both heard from holy scholars
And in true writings have read it myself,
That the perfect prince who in paradise rules
Is hostile to everything whose aim is evil,

I never saw it set down in scroll or book
That he acted with more hate against his own creation,
Avenging himself on vileness, vice or sin,
Or was more hotly angry in the haste of his purpose,

---

14. Lines 181–92 are broadly based on Galatians v, 19–21.
The poet's concentration throughout the poem is on God's vengeance for unclean life, so that he does not include in his paraphrase
the balancing passage on the fruits of the Spirit (vv. 22–3).

Or sought more suddenly to exact savage vengeance,
As when folly of fleshly filthiness was committed.
Then God, I find, forgets his gracious generosity
And fiercely takes revenge with fury in his heart.

Mark the first of foul deeds, which the false Fiend committed
While elevated high in heaven aloft,
Of all the high angels created most beautiful!
Ungratefully he regarded that gift, like a churl.[15]

He saw just himself and his sparkling looks,
And forsook his Sovereign, saying these words:
'I shall raise my royal throne in the region of the Pole-Star[16]
And be like the Lord who laid out the firmament.'

The very moment he averred it, vengeance fell upon him;
The Deity sternly doomed him, and drove him to the abyss,
With measure in his majesty, his mercy held in balance,
Diminishing his mighty dominion by but a tenth.

The Fiend, proudly fierce in the fairness of his array,
Vainglorious with the gleams of his glittering brightness,
Straight away received the sentence of God:
Thousands thronging thickly were thrown out of heaven,

Black fiends falling from the firmament on high,
Swirling at the first stroke like snow in a storm,

15. It takes a noble spirit to receive a gift graciously.
16. The word in the original for 'the Pole-star' is *tramountayne*, here used in English for the first time; the Italian word described the star seen beyond the Alps, and hence, also, for the Italians, something alien and uncivilized. The source for Lucifer's words is the well-known passage in Isaiah xiv, 13–14.

Hurled into hell-hole like a hive swarming.
For forty days the fiend folk flocked cowering[17]

Before the stinging storm stopped blowing,
But like strained meal which smokes most in a small sieve,
That horrid shower hurtling from heaven to hell
Hung all round the earth, everywhere the same:

A savage destruction, a signal vengeance.
Yet the Deity showed no dudgeon, the Devil no repentance;
Nor would he, being wilful, worship God rightly,
Nor pray to him for pity, so proud was his will.

Though violent his fall, he felt little remorse;
Though plunged in despair, he expected nothing better.
Or see the second sentence God served, on man,
Which befell through the fault of a failure in faith

When Adam the heir of happiness disobeyed.
Paradise, a place apart, was appointed for him
To live in in pleasure for a length of time
Till he should inherit that home the angels had forfeited.

But through the egging on of Eve he ate an apple
Which poisoned all people, their progeny and posterity,
Because of a decree of the Creator himself,
With a penalty put on it, to be plainly obeyed.

17. Caedmon has the devils falling for three days and nights;
Milton, presumably following Hesiod in regard to the fall of the
Titans, nine. The poet makes the period prefigure the forty days of
rain induced by God's anger with the generation of Noah.

Prohibited was the apple that Adam touched,
And our doom is the death that destroys us all.
But mild was the measure of God's manifest vengeance;
Through a matchless maiden he amended all afterwards.

God Prepares to Destroy Mankind, and Warns Noah[18]

In the third of God's thrusts all that thrived was destroyed.
There was merciless malice and mighty displeasure
At the lecherous living and looseness of the people
Who dwelt in the world and would not have masters.

They were the fairest of form and of face also,
The heartiest and happiest ever created,
The most stalwart and strong to stand upright,
And their lives lasted longer than all others'.

For they were the earliest offspring that earth had bred,
Issue of our high ancestor, Adam by name,
To whom God had granted all gainful things,
All bliss without blame that a body might have:

And likewise to the line that lived in succession.
Henceforward fairer folk would not be found again.
No law was laid down to them but to look on Nature
And keep all its courses in cleanly fulfilment.

Yet in fleshly deeds they invented filthy practices,[19]
Having new and unnatural knowledge of each other,

18. Lines 249–52 follow Genesis vi–viii.

19. To his source material in Genesis vi, 3–55, the poet seems to have applied some of the detail catalogued in Romans i, 24–32, concerning licentiousness of a much later date.

Which they wantonly used one with another,
Lusting deliberately in lawless licence.

So foul were their fleshly doings that fiends, observing[20]
Of this race how rare and ravishing were the daughters,
Fell to fornicating with them, in the fashion of humans,
And engendered giants on them with their jetting lust.

These were immoderate monsters, mighty earth-dwellers,
Far-famed for their foul and fell practices.
Love of slaughter and strife was their sign of distinction,
And the one whose wickedness was worst was called best.

Then evils in earnest spread over the world,
Multiplying many-fold among mankind,
Till the giants so jeopardized the gentle creation
That God the great maker began to be angry.

When he looked on each land, saw it lost in corruption,
And each soul forsaking the straight path of virtue,
A terrible fierce temper touched his heart,
And in inward anguish he uttered his affliction:

'The making of man I mightily repent!
I shall slaughter and destroy these sinners in their folly,
And root out of the earth all that is flesh,
Both man and beast, bird and fish.

20. Genesis vi, 4. 'The sons of God came in unto the daughters
of men.' 2 Peter ii, 4–10, and Jude, 6, refer. The fiends are the
angels who fell with Lucifer. Augustine in *De Civitate Dei*
thought angels, though spirit, could have intercourse with women,
but God's angels did not so sin. But the apocryphal Book of
Enoch mentions angels who fell because of their lust for human
women (see Gollancz, op. cit. vol. I, p. xxi and n).

'In death they shall fall down, driven from the earth.
Most sadly I sigh that I set souls there
Or ever created them! But if I do again,
I shall watch and be aware of the wickedness they do.'

There was one man who dwelled in the world at that time
Who regulated his life rightly and was readily obedient.
In dread of the Deity his days were passed,
And by going with God his grace increased:

His name was Noah, as is known well enough.
He had three sons thriving, and they three wives:
One son was Shem, the second was Ham,
And joyful-hearted Japhet was engendered third.

In the time of his temper God turned to Noah
With words of wild grief, willing bitter things:
'The end of all on the earth that are flesh
Is before my face: their fall I shall hasten.

'Their foul defilement fills me with loathing,
Their gross filth grieves me, their gleet vexes me.
I shall dispel my sorrow by destroying them all,
Living people and lands, wherever life is found.

'But build yourself a boat, I bind you to it,[21]
A container made of tree trunks, truly planed:
Construct in it stalls for savage beasts and tame,
And caulk it with clay carefully inside.

21. The Hebrew of Genesis invariably has *teva* (box, container) for the ark, which the Vulgate follows, using *arca*. (In the catacomb frescoes Noah is seen squatting in a simple square box – an *arca*). The poet is faithful to this sense, which accordingly is susceptible to the anagogical interpretation given in the Introduction (p. 52).

'Stick the joints and staple them on the outside too.
Of these dimensions make your mighty vessel:
Three hundred cubits over-all make its length,
And from side to side exactly fifty,

'And the height of the ark, have it thirty cubits,
With a widely opening window worked in the roof
A cubit across and cut exactly square.
That done, make a door that shuts down on the side.

'Have halls inside it and, everywhere, recesses,
Stables and stalls with stoutly boarded pens.
For I shall awaken a water that will wash over the world
And quell all the quick in its quivering waves.

'All that goes on foot or glides with the ghost of life urging it,
Every dweller in the world I shall do away with in my wrath.
But most clearly I shall keep this covenant with you,
Because your rule has been righteous, full of reason and
   wisdom:

'You shall enter this ark with your excellent sons
And your wedded wife:[22] with you take
The spouses of your splendid sons: this eightsome
I shall save of all souls, and destroy all the rest.

'Of each beast that bears life, bring in a pair.
Of each clean and comely kind, the couples must be seven,
But if unclean, hold only one pair.
So shall I save the seed of all separate species.

22. The appearance of this phrase in the marriage service
shows the influence of the alliterative tradition in English.

'And always match the males as mates to their own females,
Properly pairing them to pleasure each other.[23]
With all the food that can be found, fill that container;
Take sustenance for yourself and your several companions.'

The good man quickly goes to obey God's commands,
In dread sensing danger and daring to do nothing else.
The ark being framed and fashioned and fully prepared,
Then God came again, with great force speaking.

The Flood

'Now look, Noah,' said the Lord, 'Is your labour finished?
Have you caulked the ark carefully with clay everywhere?'
'Yes, Lord, by your leave,' the liege man answered,
'All is done as you ordained; I did my best.'

'Go in then,' said God, 'and get your wife in too,
Your three sons and their spouses, and say no more.
The beasts as I have bidden, bring in as well,
And when at length you are well lodged, lock yourselves in.

'In seven days I shall send with a sudden rush
A terrible tempest with torrents of rain
Which shall wash out of this world all the works of filth.
Nothing living shall I leave on the lands of Earth;

'Only the eight in this ark dwelling,
And the seed of these separate species shall I save.'
Now Noah never stopped – that night he began –
Till all were loaded and lodged, as the Lord had commanded.

23. i.e. so that they shall couple naturally, not like the fiends and
the daughters of men (ll. 269–71).

The seventh day came soon; the assembly complete,
They dwelled in the wide hold, wild and tame together.
Then the abyss burst forth, and banks of water rose;
Every spring spurted out in a spate of fury.

Every coast that kept back water was quickly submerged,
And the flowing depths were flung to the firmament above.
Many clustering clouds were cleft in shreds,
Every rift was rent and rain rushed earthwards,

Nor failed for forty days; and the flood rose,
Overwhelmed all the woods and the wide plains.
When the waters of the welkin covered the world,
All that death could draw down were drowned in them.

What a moaning was made when the mischief was known,
That death alone would not die in the deepening currents!
Waxing yet wilder, the water engulfed dwellings,
Hurled into every house, seized all the inhabitants.

At first all who could flee fled far away;
Every mother with infant ran out of her house,
Hurried to the high places, the highest there were;
Hastening to the hills, up, up they fled.

But pointless were their pains, for no pause appeared
In the torrent of the tempest, the turbulent waves,
Till every abyss was brimming, its banks overflowing,
And the dales, however deep, were drowned to the summits.

Earth's mightiest mountains no more remained dry,
Yet folk flocked to them in fear of God's vengeance;
And wild beasts from the woods on the water were floating.
Some who thought to save themselves swam vigorously,

Some strove to the summits and stared up at heaven,
Woefully waiting and whimpering with dread.
Hares and harts to the heights ran up,
Bucks, badgers and bulls to the bluffs above.

All howled in anguish to their heavenly king,
Crying to the Creator to recover them safely,
Which caused yet more chaos – his clemency was ended,
His pity departed from the people he hated.

By now the flood was flowing at their feet and still rising,
And all saw for certain they must sink in the end.
Friends clasped in fellowship, ready to fall together,
To endure their doleful destiny and die united.

The lover and his lady looked their last farewell,
Ending everything for all time, for ever parting.
When the forty days were finished, no fleshly thing moved.
For the flood had devoured all with its furious waves,

Having climbed fifteen cubits above every cliff there was,
Above the highest hill that hung over the world.
There mouldering in the mud in mighty calamity
Lay all who had heaved breath; effort was vain,

Save for the hero under hatches and his odd company,
Noah who often named the name of the Lord,
One of eight in the ark, as the high God desired,[24]
That vessel in which the various survivors stayed dry.

The ark was thrown high on the heaving currents,
Rolled close to the clouds over countries unknown.

24. In the original, the word 'eightsome' is here used for the
first time.

It weltered on the wild waters, went where it would,
Drove above the depths, in danger as it seemed,

Without means of mainmast, mizzen or bowline,
Without cable or capstan for clinging to anchors,
Or hurrock or hand-helm hooped on the rudder,[25]
Or any swaying sail for seeking a haven.

It could float only forwards as the fell winds blew,
Or waver with the water, or be washed back.
Often it rolled around, often reared on end;
Hard things would have happened, had the helmsman not
   been God.

As to the length of Noah's life, let it be truly known.
In the six hundredth year of his age, with no odd years,
On exactly the seventeenth day of the second month,
All the well-heads had weltered forth, the wide waters
   flowed;

And thrice fifty days following the flood lasted,
Every hill hidden by the heaving grey waves.
All dwellers in the world were overwhelmed by the flood,
All that floated, all that flew, all that footed the ground.

And the remnant was driven in the rack of the storm,
All kinds in the company, closely packed.
At last it was to the liking of the Lord of heaven
To remember his man in his immemorial mercy.

And he awakened a wind which wafted the waters,
Lessening the lakes that had been large before.

25. 'Hurrock', an Orkney word, apparently referring to the
after-part of the keel, inside the vessel.

Then he damned up the deep pools, sealed down the wells,
Told the rains to stop. And the tides ebbed fast,

The mighty massed main diminished and separated.
After a hundred and fifty hard days,
When that heaving ark had moved heavily about
Wherever the wind and water had hurled it,

One soft-aired day it settled, sinking to the ground,
And on a ridge of rock it rested at last
On the heights of Ararat, in hilly Armenia,
Its other name, in Hebrew, being the hill of Thanes.[26]

But though the ark was held high and dry on the crags,
The flood had not finished, or fully ebbed;
Yet the principal peaks were exposed a little,
So the bold man on board could see bare earth.

Then he opened wide his window and waved therefrom
A messenger from amongst them to make search for land.
It was the rashly proud raven, a rebel always,[27]
And coloured like coal, a canting bird.

He flew off fluttering, fanning the winds,
Soared up in the sky to search for information.
When he came to some carrion he croaked with delight;
It was decaying on a cliff that had become quite dry.

26. Thanes, a name the poet took from the French Mandeville.
It derives from *Kuh-i-Nuh*, Persian for 'Noah's Mountain'. (See
Gollancz, op. cit., vol. 1, p. 87).

27. 'Why me?' asked the raven of Noah in old legend
(Gollancz, op. cit.). Noah replied that it was unclean and otherwise useless for food or sacrifice.

And he smelled the scent of it, and swooped there at once,
Fell on the foul flesh and filled his belly.[28]
His master's command he dismissed from his mind,
He, chosen by the chieftain who had charge of the ark.

Now the raven ranged forth, recklessly uncaring
How the folk would fare provided he found food,
But the man aboard the boat who bided his return
Bitterly cursed the bird, and the beasts did as well.[29]

Noah sought another to send, and settled on the dove,
Brought on deck the bright bird, blessed her and said,
'Go, my worthy one; seek dwelling for us.
Drive over the dark water; if you hit dry land,

'Bring us word back, with bliss to us all.
Though that foul bird was false, be faithful for ever.'
To the winds she whirled away on her wings so swift,
And all day she drove on, not daring to alight.

And finding no fertile place for her foot to rest,
She circled about on the sea and searched for the ship.
As dusk came down, she descended on the ark,
And Noah caught her quickly and comfortably lodged her.

A second day he sent the dove soaring off,
Bid her fly over the flood again to find land.
And she skimmed under the sky, scouting everywhere
Till it was nearly night; then to Noah she returned.

28. Jewish and Arabic traditions have it that the raven found
carrion. A tradition drawn on by Chaucer and Gower has it that
the raven was originally white, but was turned black for its infidelity to Noah.

29. That Noah cursed the raven is an Arabic tradition.

The Disembarkation, and the Occupation of the Purified World

Over the ark one evening hovered the dove,
Then perched on the prow and patiently awaited Noah.
What! She had brought in her beak a branch of olive,
With green leaves growing graciously all over it.

That was the sign of salvation sent by our Lord,
His covenant kept with those creatures so helpless.
Where the grieving had been great, gladness now came,
And much comfort to that caulked and clinker-built ark.

Merrily on a fair morning, the month being the first
That falls in the year foremost, on the first day,
Men laughed in delight and looked out from the ark
On the waters which were waning and the world drying.

They gave glory to God, but go ashore they did not
Till the order came from him who had earlier confined them.
Then God came and gave them the gladdening word
To come up to the entrance, so that he could release them.

To the wide gate they went, and it swung open quickly.
The sons and their sire descended together,
Their wives walking with them, and the wild beasts following,
Thronging forward thickly, thrusting on their way.

But of each kind that was clean, Noah kept out one;
Then raised up an altar and hallowed it duly,
And set on it a sacrifice of every sort of creature.
That was comely and clean – God cares for nothing else.

When the beasts were blazing brightly, and the burning
   smell rose,
The savour of the sacrifice ascended to the Lord
Who succours or destroys all. He spoke to the man
In utter kindness and comfort these courteous words:

'I make known to you, Noah, I shall never again curse
The wide world entire for the wickedness of men,
For I see it is so, that the souls of men
Are thrown into thriftless error by the thoughts of their
   hearts.

'It was always so, and will ever be, from infancy onward.
The mind of man is inclined mostly to evil,
So I shall never in annoyance annihilate everything
Through loathing of man's laxity, as long as earth lasts.

'Go forth now, be fruitful, and fill the earth,
Multiply many-fold, make honour for yourself.
Seasons for you shall not cease – seed-time and harvest;
Heat and hard frost; heavy rain and drought;

'The sweetness of summer and the sorrow of winter;
The night and the day; and renewal of the year –
But shall run without rest. Rule on this earth!'
On the beasts he put his benison, and blessed earth to them.

Then they escaped and dispersed, scattering by species.
The feathered birds fluttered, flying in air,
Fish, with their fins, to the flood shot down,
Grazing beasts were gone to the grassy plains,

Wild snakes went to their dwellings in the earth,
The fox and the fitchew to the forests away,
Harts to the high heaths, hares to the gorseland,
And lions and leopards to their lake-side lairs.

Eagles and hawks to the high crags flew;
To the water went the web-footed birds.
Every beast hurried off to his own habitat,
And the four men remaining were masters of the world.

Lo! Such vengeful affliction for their vicious deeds
The Father visited on the folk of his creation:
Those whom by choice he cherished, he chastised severely,
To destroy the sinfulness that sapped his ordinances.

So beware, man, if you wish to be well thought of
In the courteous court whose King rules in bliss,
That filth of the flesh be found in you never,
Lest all the water of the world wash you in vain.

For no soul under the sun, however seemly his practice,
If sullied by sin, a single sign of filth,
But one speck of a spot will certainly rob him
Of the sight of the Sovereign who sits on high.

They shall see that show in those shimmering mansions,
Who are burnished as the beryl, bound to be pure,
Sound on every side, with no seams anywhere,
Immaculate and moteless like the margery-pearl.[30]

II

A Homily on God's Power to Detect and
Punish Lechery

Then the High King of Heaven heartily repented
That ever he gave humans earthly life:

30. The pearl is the poet's constant symbol for spiritual purity.
See index, and *Pearl* in *Medieval English Verse*, pp. 136–74.

Fierce was his revenge for man's fall into filth:
He regretted rearing man and rendering him subsistence,

When the flesh he had formed was confounded in death.
But the deed being done, he deemed it harsh,
For when sorrow, streaming, struck at his heart,
He courteously covenanted with mankind thereupon,

In the measure of his mood and the mercy of his will,
That never again for gross evil would he give man to
   slaughter,
Killing all the quick for the crimes committed,
However long the land should last in time.

No crime could cause him to cancel his covenant,
Though he did visit doom most direly at times.
Most fiercely, for the same fault, a fine kingdom he ruined
In the turbulence of his temper, terrifying many,

And all for the same evil, that infamous slimy sin,
That venom, that villainy, that vicious folly,
Which sullied man's soul and smirched his heart,
So that he was stopped from seeing his Saviour

Who hates all evils as he hates stinking hell.
Yes, nothing annoys him by night or by day
As unlawful lechery which lays waste the self.
Who shows no shame for his sin shall be killed!

But consider, man, yourself, stupid though you be!
Though you build yourself a Babel, bear it in mind
That if he who put the power to see in every piercing eye
Moved about blind himself, it would be a great wonder;

That he who fitly fashioned on the face all ears
Would be least likely to lose the power to listen.

Never trust in the truth of a tale such as that!
There is no deed so dark that he does not see it,

No sinner so sly as he sets to work
That God does not grasp it before he gives it thought.
For he is the great searching God, the ground of all action,
Scrutinizing in every soul the seat of the passions;[31]

And when he sees that all is seemly inside a man,
The heart honest and whole, he honours him then,
Sends him a solemn gift, the sight of his own face,
And painfully punishes those others, expelling them from
    earth.

But in dooming doughty men for deeds of shame,
He so abhors such sins that he is swiftly alerted:
He will suffer no stay, but slays them immediately,
As was vividly evinced by his vengeance once.

Abraham and the Angels[32]

The aged Abraham at home was sitting
Under an evergreen oak outside his door;[33]

31. The original has the common Biblical phrase 'the reins
[i.e. kidneys] and the heart' which were thought of as 'the seat of
the passions'.

32. Lines 601–1012 are based on Genesis xviii, 1–xix, 28.

33. Translators have varied in their rendering of *elonei*. The
Douai Bible, following the Vulgate, has 'vale', and the Author-
ized Version has 'plains'. Both refer to 'the tree' three verses later.
But the word means 'oaks of' (the Jerusalem Bible gives 'the Oak
at Mamre') and is indisputably plural. Possibly 'sacred trees' is
meant. At all events, the same word is used of the place where
God first appeared to Abraham in the Holy Land, Shechem
(Genesis xii, 6). The connection of the sacred tree with the divine

Brightly the sun beamed from the broad heaven
In the high heat of which Abraham was waiting;

In the shadow of the shining leaves, he shaded himself.
Three fine thriving men he saw then on the road:
If they were gracious and good, and of great beauty,
Believe me, the conclusion would most likely confirm it.

For the loyal man lying there with the leaves above him,
As soon as he saw them, swiftly advanced
And gave them such greeting as a good man gives God.
He hailed them all as one: 'Honoured Lord,

'If reward may be won by a worthless man,
I beseech you respectfully to stay for a while.
Do not pass your poor servant's place – dare I pray it? –
Without staying under this tree, taking your rest.

'And I shall bustle and bring you a basin of water
At once to wash the weariness from your feet.
Please rest on this root while I arrange immediately
To bring you some bread as balm to your hearts.'

'Proceed,' the men said, 'and seek what you suggest.
By the trunk of this spreading tree we shall attend your
    return.'
Then Abraham hurried into the house to Sarah
And ordered her to hasten, urged her to be quick:

---

manifestation is obvious. In resolving the matter, perhaps tradition
should have the last word. Abraham's Oak is still to be seen at
Mamre. Its likely age, authenticated by a forester friend of mine,
puts it in the right period; it is one of a number of ancient trees in
the region upon which primitive religion was probably centred. It
is now buttressed with concrete, and is of course a tourist attrac-
tion, being the most famous single tree in the Holy Land.

'Mix three measures of meal and make some bread,
Under hot ashes heating it quickly;
While I fetch a fattened beast, you fan the fire;
You must this very moment make a stew.'

He went blithely to the byre and brought in a calf
That was tender, not tough; told men to skin it,
And instructed his servant to stew it quickly,
And the man at his command made all ready.

Then Abraham, bare-headed, in haste prepared;
Caught up a clean cloth, cast it on the grass,
And lightly then laid on it three unleavened loaves.
By the bread he put butter which he brought next,

And due measure of milk to each man he poured,
Then placed the stew and pottage on platters of quality.
Like a steward he served them in seemly style
Both sour tastes and sweet, with such as he had;

And God, as a glad guest, made good cheer,[34]
With kind feelings for his friend, whose feast he praised.
Abraham, all hoodless, with arms uplifted,
Administered the meal to the men omnipotent.

The meal was removed; the three men remained sitting;
Then in seemly style, one spoke these words:
'Hither to your house shall I return
Before the light of your life leaves the earth.

34. The implication of Genesis xviii, 1–3, is that God is somehow implicit in 'the three men' who arrived in the heat of the day. Some commentators have seen in them an indication of the Trinity.

'Then shall Sarah conceive, and a son she shall bear
Who shall be heir to Abraham, and after his time
Gain honour and opulence and a host of nations,
And sustain the estate I have established for man.'

Then the lady, behind the door lurking, laughed in scorn,
And said slyly to herself, being Sarah the mad,[35]
'Could I truly be tickled into teeming again,
And I so old, as also is my lord?'

For truly as the Bible tells, those two were very old,
Both the lord and his lady, and their labours had not
    prospered,
For Sarah had been barren for many a bright day before,
And still stayed without seed till that same time.

Then said our Lord from his seat, 'See! So Sarah laughs,
Not taking my foretoken as true utterance!
Does she think anything can be hard for my hands to per-
    form?
I verily confirm this vow that I have made:

'I shall go, and come again, and give what I promised,
Sending your wife Sarah a son and heir.'
Then Sarah sallied forth and swore by her faith
That in spite of what they had said, she had not scoffed at all.

'Enough now, it is not so,' was the denial of the Lord,
'For you laughed, though not loudly; but let it pass.'
Then rapidly they rose, making ready to go,
And in a group together, they gazed towards Sodom.

35. There seems to be no tradition of Sarah being mad, apart
from her temerity in disbelieving God on this occasion, which
was of course celebrated in the naming of the resultant child. The
root syllable of the name 'Isaac' comes from the verb 'to laugh'.

For that city there beside them was sited in a valley
Two miles from Mamre, no more certainly.
From his dwelling the worthy man went with our Lord
To attend him with talk and tell him the way.

So God glided forth with the good man following,
Abraham with the holy ones, ushering them on
Towards the city of Sodom steeped in sin
Through the fault of filthiness. The Father threatened them,

Saying as ensues to the servant attending him:
'How can I hide my heart from Abraham the faithful,
Not tell him truly my stern intention?
He is chief father of children, so chosen by me,

'From whom races shall rise and enrich the whole world,
And blessed shall be the blood of all his line!
The burden of my burning rage I am bound to tell him;
I must open my whole purpose to Abraham at once.

Abraham Pleads for Lot

'The vile sounds of Sodom sink in my ears,
The guilt of Gomorrah goads me to anger.
I shall see for myself, by staying among the people,
If they behave as the hubbub flying up to me indicates.

'They have learnt of a lust that I little like,[36]
Having found the filthiest of fleshly perversions.

36. Lines 693–712 are an interpolation of the poet without a
strict Biblical correlative, following his paraphrase of Genesis
xviii, 20–21 in lines 685–8, but his general condemnation of
homosexual vice probably follows Romans i, 27.

Each male takes as mate a man like himself,
And they couple carnally, clasped as man and woman.

'I made them natural means, which I communicated
   secretly,
And held most holy in my ordinance for humans,
A manner of mating of marvellous sweetness.
In my brain was born the embrace of lovers:

'The modes of love I made for man's utmost delight,
That when two true ones are attached to each other,
Between the man and his mate is such mutual joy
That the purity of Paradise could prove little better;

'Provided each to each is honourably joined
By a still secret voice, unstirred by sight,
With the love-flame leaping, lashed so hot
That all the evils on earth could not quench it.

'But these have spurned my statutes, in scorn of nature,
And couple in contumely by a custom unclean.
I shall strike them sternly for their stinking filth,
As a warning to the world: let men beware for ever.'

Then Abraham was disheartened, his happiness went
As he pondered the harsh punishment promised by Our
   Lord,
And sighing, he said, 'Sire, by your leave,
Shall the sinful and the spotless suffer one penalty?

'Is it like my Lord to lay down a judgement
By which the wicked and the worthy as well shall suffer,
Venting fury on the few who never fanned your wrath?
That is hardly the habit of him who created us!

'If fifty men of virtue were found in that region
In the city of Sodom and the city of Gomorrah,
Who never flouted your law, but loved truth always,
And were righteous and reasonable, ready to serve you,

'Shall they fall through the fault and offence of others,
Receive the general judgement? What justice is that?
None that you were known for; let it not be now,
O God mild and good, and gracious of spirit!'

'For fifty,' said the Father, 'and the fair words you've spoken,
If fifty be found there not fouled by filth,
I shall forgive all their guilt through my grace alone,
And let them live unsmitten, leave them at peace.'

Then Abraham said, 'Ah! Most hallowed, most bountiful!
Holding all in your hand, both heaven and earth!
But though my say was said once, receive it not harshly
If I offer one more utterance, being but ashes and dust.

'If five of the fifty fail to be found,
But the rest be righteous, what ruling will you give?'
'If five lack of fifty,' the Father said, 'I shall free all,
And withhold my hand from harming those cities.'

'What if forty among the defiled are found to be faithful,
Will you suddenly destroy them, not reserving judgement?'
'If forty be faultless, I shall defer my vengeance,
Set aside my resentment, in spite of what I think.'

Then Abraham bowed humbly and heartily thanked him:
'Now grace be to you, God, so guileless in your wrath!

I am but evil earth and ashes muddied,
To speak with a saviour whose strength rules all!

'But I have begun to talk to God, who grants me grace,
Though in error like an idiot I answer his liberality.
If thirty fine men be found undefiled in the place,
Shall I believe that my Lord will allow them to live?'

Then God that is good gave him this answer:
'If yet thirty men throng there, I shall thrust my wrath away,
Be sparing of my spite in support of my decrees,
And put away my spleen for your pious pleading.'

'What if twenty?' said the true man, 'Will you take revenge
    then?'
'I grant them grace, since you again ask:
If those twenty be true, I shall not attack them with woes,
But pardon the whole province its poisonous crimes.'

'Now, worthy lord, one more word,' said Abraham,
'And I shall cease to strive on the side of those men.
If ten who are trustworthy be found true to your law,
Will you moderate your mood till they amend their life?'

'Granted,' said the great God; 'Gramercy,' the other,
And he stopped speaking forthwith, seeking no more.
And God glided on his way by green paths,
And only with his eyes did Abraham follow him;

And as he looked along where our Lord was passing,
He called out and cried with care in his voice:
'Mild master, if you are minded to remember me,
Then Lot, my beloved kinsman, lives in that place.

'He is settled in Sodom, and serves you humbly[37]
Among the accursed men who so mightily grieve you.
If you destroy that city, then assuage your anger,
That you may melt with mercy, and your meek servant be
    spared.'

Then he went on his way, weeping with care,
Mourning and lamenting towards Mamre's border,
And lay the livelong night, grief-laden at home,
While the Sovereign sent his spies into Sodom.

Lot Entertains the Two Angels

God's message made its way immediately into Sodom,
As that evening drew on, with two handsome angels,
Moving together modestly like merry young men.
There Lot all alone leaned on his door,

At a porch of his palace placed by the gates,
A place rich and royal like the man of rank himself.[38]
As he stared into the street where stalwarts were at sport,
He saw the splendid pair swiftly advancing:

Brave men were they both, with beardless chins[39]
And lovely waving locks gleaming like raw silk;
Like the bloom of the briar-rose their bare skin showed;
Unclouded were their countenances, and clear their eyes,

37. When Abraham and Lot arrived in the land, 'Lot chose
him all the plain of Jordan' (Genesis xiii, 11).

38. Lot is wealthy only by implication in the Bible (Genesis
xiii, 6), where his substance is pastoral, consisting of herds. A
Rabbinical tradition has it that he hesitated to leave Sodom because of his wealth.

39. The beauty of the angels is a Platonic addition of the poet's.

And the white clothes they wore most worthily suited them.
Faultless of feature and form were both,
With everything in harmony – after all, they were angels.
Lot swiftly understood this, sitting in his doorway.[40]

He rapidly rose and ran to meet them,
With low bow saluted them, low to the ground,
And solemnly said, 'Sirs, I beseech you
To delay at my lodging and linger here.

'Enter your servant's house, I humbly beg you.
Let me fetch you a vessel for your feet to be washed.
I ask you to house with me for only one night,
And in the merry morning, you may go your way.'

But they said they had no desire to sleep indoors,
But in the street where they stood would stay quietly,
And lie the night long lodging out of doors,
For the heavens on high were house enough for them.

Lot urged them so long, imploring them courteously,
That they agreed to go in, and gainsaid him no more.
The bold man brought them quickly into the building,
Which was royally arrayed, for he was a rich man.

Lot's wife gave them welcome as well as she could,
And his two dear daughters deferentially greeted them.
Demure were these maidens, not married as yet,
Seemly and sweet, and extremely well dressed.

40. Gollancz (op. cit., vol. i, p. xxvi and n.) notes that Lot, like Abraham before him (l. 612), recognizes the quality of his visitants, and instructs his wife not to offer them leaven (l. 820), because it would set up fermentation, and so corrupt their pure essence.

CLEANNESS

Then Lot alertly looked about him
And admonished his men to make ready a meal:
'But see that all you offer is wholly unleavened,
For neither sour yeast nor salt shall be served to my guests.'

Yet it seems that his spouse was scornfully defiant,
And softly said to herself: 'Insensitive fellows
To hate salt in their sauce: they seem not to care
That others go without it, the ill-bred pair.'

Then she seasoned the sauce with salt for each of them,
Gainsaying the specific instruction of her lord,
Serving them in scorn, secure in her skill.
Why such folly, poor fool? She made God furious with
     her.[41]

Then they sat down to supper and were served promptly:
The guests in good mood, most gaily conversing,
Blithe and lovely till at last they washed[42]
And the tables and trestles were tilted against the wall.

After supper when they'd sat for a space of time,
Still not ready for sleep, the city surged up.
All who could wield weapons, the weaker and stronger,
Had come to Lot's castle to carry off the men;

They clustered in crowds, crammed in the gateway.
The guard gave the alarm and a great outcry arose
As they cudgelled and clubbed the enclosing walls.
Then shrilly and sharply, they shouted these words:

41. A typically priestly anti-feminism seems to motivate the
poet, who makes great play of the failure of two women, Sarah and
Lot's wife, to participate in the harmony of God's way.
42. It was good manners in medieval times to wash after meat,
rather than before.

'If you love your life, Lot, living here,
Turn over to us those two you're entertaining
For a little love-learning, for our lust demands
They submit to Sodom's manners, as men must who pass
   through.'

What! They spat out and spewed such scandalous words!
What! they bawled and boasted of such abominable
   obscenity
That the wind and the weather and the world still stink
Of the filth and defilement their foul words raised.

Then Lot looked up, alarmed at the din,   [heart,
And sharp shame shot through him, and he shrank at the
For he was aware of the wicked ways of Sodomites:
No grief had ever grated so gravely on his mind.

'Alas!' then said Lot, and lithely he rose,
Going to the broad gateway after getting up from the bench.
What! he feared not the fury of those filthy knaves,
But passed through the portal to the peril that awaited.

He went out of the wicket gate and swung it shut,
And it clicked and clanged as it closed behind him.
Then mildly and with measure to those men he spoke,
Hoping to lessen their lechery by his lofty courtesy.

'Oh my fair friends, you follow strange customs!
Cease this dreadful din, do not discommode my guests.
Fie on your defilement, which fouls your good selves!
You are jolly gentlemen indeed, but your japes are unseemly.

'Let me teach you a trick more temptingly natural:
I've a treasure in my tall house, two fair daughters,
Maidens immaculate, knowing no man as yet:
In Sodom, though I say it, are no seemlier girls.

'Full-grown and ripe are they, ready to be mastered;
To play with such pretty ones would please you more.
I will give you the two girls so gracious and lively;
Pleasure in them as you like, but leave my guests alone.'

Then those rioting ribalds raised such a roar
That their dreadful dissoluteness deafened him almost.
'Do you forget that you're favoured as a foreigner to live here?
A stranger, a serf, we'll strike off your head!

'Who enjoined you to judge our japes with your censure,
You who came as a country boy, and now call yourself
   rich?'
Then they thrust forward and thronged about him
And seriously distressed him, sorely pressing him;

But the alert young men lithely leaped forward,
Whipped open the wicket gate and went to him,
Took hold of his hand, hurried him in,
And bolted and barred the gates with big battens.

Then with a spell they struck those swarming people,
So that they blundered about as blind as Bayard,[43]
Failed to find the front of Lot's house,
And knocked about all night for nothing in the end.

Then each man went off, his ardour unsatisfied,
And roamed disgruntled to whatever rest he could get.
But the people in that place were peremptorily woken
By the ugliest ill-hap ever suffered on earth.

43. Bayard was the legendary horse of Charlemagne. 'Legend
relates that he is still alive and can be heard neighing in the
Ardennes on Midsummer Day' (*Brewer's Dictionary of Phrase and
Fable*, p. 106). Bayard was recklessly brave, hence the association
with blindness, as in the phrase 'as bold as blind Bayard'.

CLEANNESS

The Destruction of the Cities of the Plain

The dark of the deep night was done at last,
And ruddy and red arose the dayspring.
Very early the angels roused their host,
And greatly zealous in God's cause, got him up.

And Lot leaped up, alarmed in his heart.
They told him tersely to take what he wanted,
'With your lady wife and slaves and lovely daughters;
For we plead with you, Lot, to let your life be saved.

'Fly fast from this foul place, before you are destroyed,
Quickly with all your court till you come to a hill.
Go fast on your feet, facing to your front,
And never be so bold as to look back once.

'Let your steps not stumble, but stride on rapidly
Until you reach a refuge, not resting at all.
For we shall ruin the whole region, raze everything,
Make all its vile villains vanish in a flash,

'Have the land and those alive there lost together.
Sodom shall suddenly sink into the earth,
The foundations of dark Gomorrah dive into hell,
And the whole range of the realm rumble down into
    rubble.'

Then loudly said Lot, 'Lord what is best?
If I fly on foot, in fleeing for safety,
How shall I hide from him whose rage
Beats in his breath that burns everything?

'How creep to escape my Creator's wrath,
Whose fury may follow me, striking in front or behind?'

'No anger,' said the angel, 'has the High King for you;
His esteem has saved you from those sinners' fate.

'Now pick out a place that will proffer you shelter,
And he who sent us will spare it for your sake
Because you're strangely yourself still, though sin surrounds
    you,
And because Abraham your uncle asked it himself.'

'Do so,' said the splendid man, 'and stop not at all,
But gather together those who are to go with you
And keep on your course, not casting a backward glance,
For the city shall be destroyed before the sun has risen.'

Said Lot, 'May the Lord aloft be praised!
There is a city called Zoar beside this valley;
On a round hill which rears there, it is raised above.
I would, if it were his wish, willingly escape there.'

Lot woke his wife and his well-favoured daughters,
Besides two men whom he meant to marry those maidens,
But they took it as a trick and hardly attended to him;
Though Lot urgently implored them, they lay quite still.

The angels hurried on the others with threats,
And forced them all four forth from the portal.
There was Lot, his beloved wife, and his lovely daughters;
Not a single other soul in the five cities would they save.

The angels led them by hand out at the gates,
Instructed them to travel fast, and told them of the danger:
'Lest you be caught in the carnage with these criminals here,
Seize your own safety, go swiftly away!'

They paused not to parley, but peremptorily fled;
And early, before heaven was gleaming, to a hill they came.
Then the great fury of God began in the upper air:
He awoke the winds to make wild weather,

And they rushed upwards raging, wrestling together,
From the four ends of the firmament in frenzied uproar.
Clouds clustered between them, cast up towers
Which the thrust of thunderbolts often went through;

The rain rattled down, riddled thickly
With fell flashes of fire and flaming sulphur,
All smouldering in smoke, and smelling horribly.
This storm struck Sodom suddenly from all sides;

It gushed over Gomorrah, so that the ground dissolved,
Into Admah and Zeboim, so that all four cities[44]
Were drenched by the rain, and roasted and burned,
And horror struck all the inhabitants they had.

For when hell heard the hounds of heaven[45]
It was grisly glad, and grinding apart
The great bars of the abyss, it burst swiftly upwards,
Ripping open the region with rifts most terrible.

Then crags and cliffs were cloven in shreds
Like loose leaves of a book that flutter about.
The stinking storm of brimstone had stopped by this,
And the cities with their suburbs were sunk in hell;

44. Admah and Zeboim are traditionally located under the Dead Sea.

45. Gollancz (op. cit., vol. 1, p. 93) thinks the poet has in mind the 'Gabriel hounds', 'a name popularly in Lancashire and elsewhere in the North assigned to what is supposed to be a spectral pack, whose yelping cries betokened approaching death and disaster'.

The people penned in them were in pain and leaderless,
Knowing of the annihilation which none could escape.
So huge was the uproar of their howls of misery
That it clattered in the clouds for Christ to have mercy.

And Lot was listening as he climbed up to Zoar.
And the women who went the same way heard too,
Their flesh full of fear as they fled on together,
At the double, in dread, never daring to look back.

Lot and those lily-whites, his two lovely daughters,
Ever followed as they faced, their eyes fixed forwards.
But the luckless lady who was lax in obedience,
To glimpse the great destruction, glanced at the cities

Looking over her left shoulder. Lot's contrary wife
Just blinked backwards, and in barely a moment
She was standing stone-still, a stark statue,
As salt as any sea: and she stands there yet.

Her companions went past, not pausing or noticing,
Then safely in Zoar, they sat down and blessed God;
With pure love uplifted, they lauded him greatly
Who had considered his servants and saved them from woe.

All the damned were now drowned, the deed was done,
In panic the people of the little place had rushed out[46]
And sinking in the charmed sea, were swiftly killed.
So only Zoar was saved, being set on a hill,

And the three people there, Lot and his lovely daughters.
For his mate was missing, on the mountain abandoned,
A statue of stone with a salty taste,
Having been found unfaithful for faults of two kinds:

46. 'Zoar' means 'little'.

One, she served salt at supper before the Lord;
Two, she blinked a look backwards, though forbidden to
   do so.
She stands as stone for one, and salt for the other,
And they like to lick her, the living beasts of the plain.

Abraham was up early in the morning,
Having had anguish in his heart the whole night long,
In solicitude for Lot lying awake:
Then he climbed to where he had left Our Lord before.

And ever his eyes looked over to Sodom,
One of the sweetest cities ever seen on earth,
As a dependency of Paradise planted by God;
Now plunged in a pit, as if packed in with pitch.

Such redness of reeking smoke rose from the black,
Such ashes flew up in the air, such embers,
As when fiery furnaces fling up foaming slag,
Fed by brilliant brands burning underneath.

It was a violent vengeance that devoured those places,
Made such fine towns and folk founder utterly.
Where five cities once stood a sea now extends,[47]
A sea dark and dreary, to death devoted,

Livid, bubbling and black, and bad to be near,
A stinking cesspit which destroyed sin,
Foetid and foul, offensively smelling.
So 'the Dead Sea' men deem it, dark for ever,

47. Mandeville (*Travels*, ed. Malcolm Letts, Hakluyt Society, 1954, ch. 13) mentions five cities. In addition to Sodom, Gomorrah and Zoar, which are named in Genesis 18–19, there are Admah and Zeboiim.

Because what death has done endures there still;
And it is broad and bottomless, and bitter like gall,
And things living cannot lie for long in that lake,
And it kills all the coasts it comes to touch.

For lay thereon a lump of lead, it will float,
And lay a light feather, it will lie under water;
And where that water wets the earth
Nothing green can grow, neither grass nor plant.

If a murderer heaves a man in, meaning to kill him,
Though he lie in that loathsome lake for a month,
He must linger in that lake in everlasting perdition,
And never lose his life till the last day of the world.[48]

Its creation is accursed, and its coasts as well:
The clay that clings to it is caustic and corrosive,
Both its alum and bitumen are bitter and acrid,
The sulphur is sour and so is the glass-gall.[49]

And there washes in that water, in waxen lumps,
Effervescent asphalt as offered by spicers.
Such is all the soil beside that sea,
Which foully gnaws the flesh and festers the bones.

And there are trees by that tarn, of a treacherous kind,
Which burgeon and bear most beautiful blossoms,
And the fairest fruit that can be found on earth,
As orange, or other fruit, or even pomegranate,

48. The body floats for ever, and hence never obtains final rest. Lines 1022–48 are based on Mandeville.
49. Sandiver, or glass-gall. 'Liquid, saline matter found floating on glass after vitrification' (*Shorter Oxford English Dictionary*).

So ruddy and ripe and richly coloured
That a man might imagine it a marvellous dainty.
But when it is bruised, or broken, or bitten open,
There's no sweetness or worth, just winnowing ashes.

A Homily on Cleanness

All these are tokens and types to turn over in the mind,
Bespeaking sinful behaviour and the ensuing vengeance
Our Father sent forth on the filth of that nation.
By this lore man may learn that he loves virtue;

And if our courteous Lord cares for clean behaviour,
And you crave to come to his court at the last,
To see the Saviour enthroned and his sweet face,
I can give no clearer counsel than: be clean always.

For Clopinel in depicting his perfect Rose[50]
Expressively puts it, to him who would prosper
In loving a lady: 'Closely study her,
How she behaves, and what attitude she approves:

And follow in the footsteps of the fair one you love.
And faithfully follow the fair one you praise.
This do, and though she deal you disdain at first,
At last she will love you for your likeness to herself.'

Likewise, if you lay claim to the love of God,
And loyally love him with a liegeman's devotion,

---

50. In lines 1057–68, the poet is drawing on 'Le Roman de la
Rose' (ll. 8021–38), which in its turn derives from Ovid. An
interesting application of religious allegory to the literature of profane love.

Then copy the cleanness of Christ, whose purity
Is perfectly polished, like the pearl itself.[51]

Look how he first alit in that loyal maiden,
In how comely a casket he was enclosed there,
When no virgin was violated, no violence done,
But her body the more brightly pure for bearing God.

And in Bethlehem the blessed, when he was born afterwards,
In what purity they parted in spite of the poverty!
No bower was more blissful than that byre then,
No castle more courtly than that cattle-shed,

No girl under God with so glad cause to groan.
There the sickness was salved that seemed sorest,
The rose-scent rioted where rank rotting had been,
Solace and song where sorrow had lamented:

For angels with instruments, such as harps and pipes,[52]
Royally ringing rebecks, the resonant fiddle,
And all pleasant things that properly might please the heart
Delighted my Lady at her delivery time.[53]

The gentle babe was born burnished so pure
That ox and ass both humbly bowed to him,
For such cleanness could come only from the King of
    nature:
No cleaner one came from such an enclosure before.

51. The pearl of great price (Matthew xiii, 45–6) is a symbol of
Christ.

52. The accompaniment of divine music, the homage of the
animals, the painless birth itself, derive from chapter xiv of the
Pseudo-Matthew.

53. The painless delivery of Christ was one of the Five Joys of
the Virgin Mary.

So coming thence cleanly, and being courteous thereafter,
He utterly abhorred all things wicked;
With his noble nature he would never touch
Anything that was evil or inwardly filthy.

Yet there limped to him the loathly, lazars for example,
The lepers, the lame, those who lurched in their blindness,
The poisoned, the paralysed, those putrefying in fever,
The dried-up, the dropsical, and the dead lastly.

All called on that courteous one and claimed his grace.
He gave them cures graciously, and granted their prayers;
Every time he touched them, he turned them healthy
More quickly and cleanly than craft of medicine.

His handling was so holy, all ordure shunned it;
So good the gracious touch of the God and man,
So fine the force of his fingers that he found,
When cutting or carving, no call for a knife,[54]

And broke the bread without blade accordingly,
For in fact his fair hands more finely cut it,
More smoothly and skilfully sundered the bread,
Than all the tools of Toulouse could attempt to carve it.[55]

So clean is he and scrupulous whose court you seek:
How can you come to his kingdom unpurified?

54. Gollancz (op. cit., vol. 1, p. xvii) notes several medieval
references to this legend, which developed from Luke xxiv, 35.
Christ transcends the requirement of medieval etiquette, which
was that bread should be cut, not broken.

55. Since there appears to have been no cutlery industry at
Toulouse, Gollancz (ibid.) is probably right in suggesting that
there was a confusion with 'Toledo' at some point.

Since we are all sinful and suffering and vile,
How shall we hope to behold him enthroned?

Yes, that Master is merciful, though mire and muck
Defile you with filth while you fare through life.
Yet you may shine after shrift, though shame once held you,
And be purified by penance, be a pearl of God.

The pearl is praised as priceless among precious stones,
Though its cost in coin is not accounted the highest.
What quality causes this but its colour of purity,
That wins her honour above all other white stones?

For she shines so shimmering, is shaped so round,
Being faultless and flawless – if she is fine indeed –
That however aged or much-handled she becomes,
The pearl is not impaired while proudly esteemed;

But if by chance things change and she be cherished no
   more,
Her brightness becoming blurred in the box where she lies,
Then but wash her in wine, worthily, as is due,
And by her quality she will become cleaner than before.

So if people are poisoned by opprobrious deeds,
And their souls are sullied, they may seek shrift
And be polished by the priest, when penance is done,
Brighter than the beryl or braided pearls.

But beware, when you're washed in the water of shrift,
And polished like parchment that's perfectly scraped,
That you stain your soul with sin no more,
For your misdoing will then double the disdain of the Lord,

Raising his wrath more rapidly than ever,
His anger much hotter than if you had not washed.
For when a soul is sealed and sanctified as God's,
He holds it wholly his, and have it he will;

But if it reverts to vice, he violently resents it,
As a wrongful robbery, a raid by a thief.
Be vigilant against his vengeance; very angry is God
With those who gainsay his grace and go back to filth.[56]

Though it be but a basin, a bowl or cup,
A small plate or salver that has served God once,
He forbids it to be flung in defilement to the ground,
So abhorrent of evil is the ever-righteous.

This was brought out in Babylon, in Belshazzar's time,
Whom misfortune fell on with furious suddenness,
For he fouled and defiled the vessels of the Temple,
Which had served the Sovereign some time before.

If I may take up your time, I shall tell the tale
How much more sadly he suffered for scorning to respect
   them
Than his forsaken father who forcibly stole them,
Robbing the right religion of its relics.[57]

56. This argument that the sin of a backslider is worse than the sin of one who has never known the grace of God is important to the poet in his developing concept of consecration.

57. 2 Chronicles xxxvi, 18.

III

The Capture of Jerusalem

Daniel set it down in his dialogues once,[58]
(And expressly proved it in his prophecies as well)[59]
How the gentry of the Jews and Jerusalem the noble
Were savagely destroyed and struck to the ground

When the folk were found to be false to their faith
Who had held to the high God, to be his for ever;
For he had given them his grace, and greatly helped them
In the marvellously many mischiefs they had suffered.

But they were false to their faith and followed other gods;
Which aroused his wrath, and raised it so high
That he fortified those faithful to the false religion
To make those false to the true faith fall in destruction.

This was certainly seen when Zedekiah reigned[60]
In Judah, a judge of the Jewish kings,
Who sat on Solomon's throne in solemn state,
And neglected his loyalty to the Lord of courtesy,

Embracing abominations and bowing to idols,
Caring little for the laws whose liegeman he was.
So our Father provoked a fierce foeman,
Nebuchadnezzar, who noxiously harmed him.

58. The poet in fact bases this section on Jeremiah lii, 1–26.
59. Gollancz suggests (op. cit., vol. i, p. 95) that 'dialogues'
refers to Daniel i–vi, and 'prophecies' to chs. vii–xii.
60. 2 Chronicles xxxvi, 12–14.

He pressed into Palestine with proud men in plenty,
And wasted with war the dwellings and towns.
He harried all Israel and carried off the best,
But the gentry of Judah in Jerusalem he besieged,

Surrounding the ramparts with his resolute men,
At every gate a gallant captain, girding them round,
For a bastion embattled about was that city,
Stocked with stalwart men to withstand a siege.

Then the assault on the besieged city started,
Swift skirmishes spread, and slaughter began.
Battering at each bridge was a big siege tower,
From which were sent seven assaults each day.

On the towers contended intrepid warriors,
And on breastworks of boards too, built on the walls.[61]
They fought and fended off and fell locked together;
But the town was never taken in two years of war.

At last, after a long time, the luckless defenders
Found food was failing, and famine spread.
The hot hunger within hurt them far more
Than assaults from the besiegers who stayed outside.

The people were in despair in the proud city,
For meat was missing, and men became feeble;
They were so firmly confined, they could find no way
To forage for food, one foot from the fortress.

61. In the Middle Ages temporary wood breastwork was sometimes built on to battlements, to accommodate soldiers who, from such a platform, could prevent besiegers scaling or undermining the walls of a castle or town.

Then the king of that company called a council
And planned with his paladins a piece of trickery:
They stole out in the still night, not setting off one shout,
And hurried through the host before the enemy knew of it.

But the watchman beyond the wall was not outwitted by
    this,
And his clamorous call cleft the sky:
A loud alarum was let fly on the plain.
Warriors roused from their rest ran to their armour,

Heaved on their helmets, to horse leaped,
And clear clarion calls cracked in the air.
The enemy army, hurling fast onwards,
Followed the fleeing host, found them quickly,

Overtook them in no time, tore them from saddle,
And each prince had his peer prone on the ground.
The king was caught by the Chaldean princes,
The gentry were jerked off their horses on Jericho's plains,

And proffered as prisoners to that powerful prince,
Nebuchadnezzar, most noble on throne.
And he was most happy, his enemies in his power!
He spoke to them despitefully, and spilled their blood after-
    wards.

He slew each king's son in the sight of his father,
With great grimness gouged out his eyes,
Had him brought to Babylon, the beautiful city,
And thrown down in a dungeon, to endure his fate.

Now see how the Sovereign disposed his vengeance!
Not for Nebuchadnezzar, nor for his nobles,
Was Zedekiah so savagely struck in his pride,
But for being so bad in his bearing to the Lord.

For had the Father stayed friendly who before had guided
   him
(Him the traitor who in trespass turned to other gods),
Too cold would be all Chaldea and the countries of India,
And Turkey too, to trouble the Jews much.

Yet Nebuchadnezzar would not go away
Till he had overturned the town and torn it to the ground.
He ordered a high-born officer to Jerusalem,
Whose name was Nebuzardan, to annihilate the Jews.

He was a master of men and mighty himself,
The chief of the chivalry, in charge of assaults.
He broke down the barriers, and the battlements next,
Then entered in eagerly, with ire in his heart.

What! A tiny triumph, for the troops were away,
The good ones all gone with the governor of the city.
And the men who remained were so miserably starved,
One woman would have been worth the most warrior-
   like four.

Nevertheless Nebuzardan spared no one for that,
But put all the inhabitants to the edge of the sword.
They slaughtered the sweetest seemly maidens,
Spilled the brains of babies, and bathed them in blood.

Priests and prelates they pressed to death,[62]
And the wombs of wives and wenches they cut open
So that their bowels bubbled about in the ditches;
And they took care to kill all that they could catch.

---

62. In order to avoid spilling the blood of God's anointed? But
see sixteen lines further on.

Yet some escaped the savage sweeps of their swords:
They were trussed and tied on steeds quite naked,
Their feet fettered and fastened under the horses' bellies,
And brutally brought to Babylon to suffer.

So they sat in slavery, the sometime noble;
Now changed to churls, and charged with drudgery
Like carrying, pulling carts, and milking cows,
Who had lately been lords and ladies, lounging in palaces.[63]

The Holy Ornaments and Vessels of the Temple are Taken to Babylon[64]

Nebuzardan even now would not stop,
But took all his troops to the Temple precinct;
There they beat on the bars, burst open the gates,
With one surging rush slew all who served there,

Held the priests by the hair and hacked off their heads,
Did deacons to death, struck down the clerks,
And all the maidens of the minster they murdered atrociously[65]
In the swath of the swords that destroyed them all.

63. Standard medieval Wheel of Fortune stuff this; like Chaucer's Monk's definition of tragedy, which concerns

> 'hym that stood in greet prosperitee,
> And is yfallen out of heigh degree
> Into myserie, and endeth wrecchedly'.

64. A division not given by Gollancz.

65. A nice instance of the poet's happy habit of seeing the Old Testament world through medieval Christian eyes. 'Maidens of the minster' indeed!

Then, raging robbers, they ran to the relics,
Pillaged all the ornaments the holy place had –
The pillars of pure brass painted with gold,
The chief chandelier, which charged the place with light,[66]

Bearing aloft the lamp which glowed everlastingly
Before the Holy of Holies, where miracles happened.
They cast down the candlestick, and the crown as well
That the altar had upon it, of heavy rich gold,

The silver gilt goblets and gridirons too,
The bright pillar bases and beautiful bowls,
The huge platters and precious plates of gold,
The vials and vessels full of virtuous gems.

Now has Nebuzardan taken all these noble things,
Pillaged the precious place, packed its riches.
All the gold in the offertory, a huge amount,
With the urns of the holy place, in hampers he placed.

Swiftly and despitefully he sacked the place
Which Solomon in such long years had sought to establish
With all the cunning of his craft, with clean conscience
    working,
Devising the vessels and the vestments so pure.

With the skill of his science, for his Sovereign's love,
The house and its ornaments he enhanced all together.
That treasure now is taken in a trice by Nebuzardan,
The city and its sanctuary destroyed and burnt to ashes.

Then he laid waste the land with legions of horsemen,
Harrying Israel's every corner,
Then, his chariots well charged, he found his chieftain
And carried to the king his captured booty,

66. The 'chandelier' presumably refers to the Menorah.

And presenting him with prisoners as spoils of war –
Many worthy men while their world lasted,
Many a mighty man's son, and maidens most noble,
The proudest of the province, and prophets' children,

Hananiah, Azariah, and also Michael,
And Daniel devoted to dream divination –
More than a multitude of proud mothers' sons.
Nebuchadnezzar was now most happy,

Having conquered the king and captured the country,
Destroyed all the sternest and strongest in arms,
Laid their leaders of law to the ground,
And made prisoners of the prominent prophets of the land.

Most jocund was his joy at the jewellery so splendid,
When it was shown him shimmering, to his sharp
    wonder,
For Nebuchadnezzar had never known till then
Of vessels and valuables so vastly precious.

Seizing them solemnly, he spoke praise to the Sovereign
Who was high lord of all, Israel's God;
Such a god, such a good man, such glorious vessels,
Never came out of one country to Chaldea's realms.

He stowed them in his treasury in a well-tried place
Royally and with reverence, as was right and proper,
Behaving afterwards, as you shall hear, wisely,
For worse fate might have befallen him, had he undervalued
    them.

That king reigned most royally for the rest of his life:
As conqueror of every coast he was called Caesar,
Emperor of the whole Earth, and also the Sultan;
And his great name was engraved as god of the ground,

Through the discourse of Daniel, who drew him to under-
   stand
That all good comes from God, and gave him examples,
So that he caught the whole consequence clearly in the end
And often manifested his mastery with more meekness.

But all are drawn direly to death in the end;
However lofty a lord be, he falls low to the ground.
And so Nebuchadnezzar, as needs must be,
For all his grand government, in the ground lies buried.[67]

But then the bold Belshazzar, his first-born son,[68]
Was installed in his stead, and established his rule.
Boldest and best in Babylon he thought himself,
Having on earth and in heaven no peer.

For he began in the glory the great man had left,
Nebuchadnezzar, his noble father;
No king of Chaldea had become so powerful,
But he honoured not the high king who holds sway in
   heaven,

Only false phantoms, fiends made by hand
With tools out of hard trees, and tilted upright.
Stocks and stones he called strong gods,
When gilded with gold and engraved with silver;

He crawled to them crying, calling for help.
If good advice was given, he promised them great rewards,
But when their grace was not granted, he was goaded to rage,
Clutched a huge club and clouted them to bits.[69]

67. The Wheel of Fortune philosophy again. See note 63.
68. Lines 1333–1812 are based on Daniel v.
69. Perhaps the poet is echoing the fine scorn of idol-worship
expressed in Baruch vi, and Wisdom xiii–xiv.

Thus vaunting and vain his vile rule continued,
In lust and lechery and loathsome deeds.
A winsome wife, a worthy queen, he had,
But also many mistresses, whom he miscalled ladies.

With his splendid strumpets and strange dressings-up,
His love of quaint cooking and curious perversions,
The mind of that man was all on monstrous things – [70]
Till the Sovereign of the sky decided to change matters.

Belshazzar's Feast

Now this bold Belshazzar bethought himself once
Of revealing his vainglory in vicious display:
His follies and foulness did not suffice the man,
But all the world must witness his wicked deeds.

In Babylon Belshazzar began to proclaim,
And through the country of Chaldea the call reverberated,
For the gathering together of the great of the land,
An assembly on a certain day for the Sultan's feast.

To make that mighty meal all men were advised
That the king of every country should come thither,
Every chief with his chivalry and his champion warriors,
All coming to court to declare their allegiance,

To reverence him rightly and attend his revels,
And bow low to his lovers with 'my lady' on their lips.
To praise his royal splendour, many princely men came,
Many a bold baron to Babylon the great.

[70]. Like the antediluvian sinners of lines 265–76. Apart from
tippling from the Temple vessels, the only misdemeanour of
Belshazzar mentioned in the Bible is the possession of concubines.

To Babylon so many bold men beat their steps,
Coming to the court, staunch kings and emperors,
And lords of many lands, with ladies in train,
That to name the number is well-nigh impossible.

That splendid city was of stupendous size;
No seemlier site existed under the stars,
For proudly on a level plain, it was perfectly placed,
With seven wide streams swirling about it,

And a wonderful wall, worked to the top
With clever carving and crowned with battlements,
And towers of pinnacles between, twenty spears' length high,
Topped by platforms of planks and palisades thwartwise.[71]

The palace on that part of the plain enclosed,[72]
In length and breadth alike, was quadrilinear,
Each side stretching seven miles on the ground,
And in the centre was set the Sultan's throne.

It was a palace to be proud of, surpassing all others
For the wonder of its work and the walls enclosing it.
Recessed within the hall, high houses were built;
In the archways that held them up horses could run.

When it was near the announced time for the noble feast to
    start,
Duly on the dais the dukes came together,

71. As in Jerusalem; see note 61.
72. Gollancz (op. cit., vol. 1, p. xxvi) notes that this description is reminiscent of that of the Great Khan's court in Mandeville's *Travels*, ch. 24.

And up the steep stairway of the great stone platform[73]
Belshazzar was borne boldly to his throne.

The floor of the fair hall was filled with knights then,
Striding to the side-tables to seek seats there,
For on the dais of honour were only the high king
And his proud paramours in their pretty clothes.

When the guests were graciously seated, the feast began in
    earnest.
Stentorian trumpets startled the hall
And the blast of their din bounced back from the walls;
They dangled broad banners brilliant with gold.

The roast was borne to the banquet on broad platters
Of scintillating silver, and served with sauces.
The lids were high houses, the upper parts carved,
But pared in paper painted in gold,[74]

Showing fierce baboons above and beasts below,
And fair birds in the foliage fluttering between
In azure and indigo highly enamelled:
On horseback they offered it all and thence served it.

Came the kettledrums' clatter and the cries of pipes,
Timbrels and tabors in a tumult of noise;
Cymbals and zithers spoke their reply
With battering and banging of beating drumsticks.

Everyone in the hall was often served again,
Gladly receiving the several courses in sight of the dais,

73. This resembles the description in Mandeville (*Travels*, ch. 24) of Prester John 'going up to meat'.

74. A typical 'table subtlety' of the fourteenth century, a decoration for the delight of guests, is now described.

Where the lord and all his lovers leaned on the tables.
So well they plied him with wine, it warmed his heart,

Beat up into his brain and unbalanced his mind,
Weakening his wits till he went sottish;
For he squinted goggling and stared at the strumpets beside
   him
And all the bold barons on benches by the walls.

Then insane disorder seized his heart,
And a wicked whim welled up in his mind.
The master commanded his marshal to approach,
And told him to take the treasure-chests, unlock them

And fetch out the vessels his father had brought,
Nebuchadnezzar, noble in strength,
Who had taken them from the Temple in his triumph of
   arms,
In Judah, in Jerusalem, but gently cared for them.

'Bring them to my board, brimful of drink
And let these ladies lap from them – I love them dearly!
I shall courteously make clear, and they shall quickly see,
That no baron shows bounty better than Belshazzar.'

The treasurer was told his instructions at once,
Caught up his keys and unlocked the caskets and coffers.
Many bright burdens were brought into hall;
Comely white cloths covered many sideboards,

And splendidly set at the sides of the hall
Were the jewels of Jerusalem, gems of brilliance.
The high bronze altar was eased into position,
And the great crown of gold raised gloriously on top of it:

It had been blessed of old by bishops' hands
And with the blood of beasts in benison anointed –
A solemn sacrifice with sweet savour
Before the high one of heaven, to honour him.

Now it was set to serve Satan, the black fiend,
Before the bold Belshazzar with bragging and vainglory.
High on this altar was heaved this noble vessel
Which had been cunningly carved with curious craft.

Solomon had striven for seven years and more
With all the science sent him by our sovereign Lord
To fashion and form those vessels faultlessly.
There were brilliant bowls of clear burnished gold

Enamelled highly with azure, and ewers the same,
Chaste cups with covers, of castle's shape[75]
With beautiful buttresses beneath their battlements,
And figures filed into fantastic forms;

The covers of the cups which crowned the rims
Were skilfully sculpted as slender turrets,
With pinnacles plainly placed between,
And all embossed above with branches and leaves,

In which parrots and magpies were depicted perched
As if proudly pecking at pomegranates;
And all the blossoms on the bough were blushing pearls,
And all the fruits were formed of flashing gems,

Sapphire and sard, scintillating topaz,
Almandine and emerald, and amethystine stones,

75. Gollancz notes that censer-covers like this existed in medieval times (op. cit., vol. 1, pp. xxvi–viii).

Chalcedony, chrysolite and clearest rubies,
Peridots and pynkardines, but always pearls amongst them;[76]

The brims of the beakers and bowls were all
Trailing with trefoils set transversely.
The golden goblets were engraved all round,
The incense phials fretted with flowers and golden
    butterflies.

Upon that high altar, all was arrayed alike.
The candelabrum was carried there quickly by a contrivance;
The perfect adornment of its pillars was praised by many,
So were the bases of brass that bore up the whole,

And the bright boughs above it, braided with gold,
And the blossoming branches on them, and birds perching[77]
Of many curious kinds, quaint in hue,
As if they had winged upon the wind, waving their feathers.

Lambent in the bower-leaves, lamps were arrayed
And other lovely lights that gleamed in beauty;
Candlesticks with wide cups for catching wax
With beasts of burning gold, bordered the base.

It was not wont to waste wax in that hall,[78]
But in the temple of truth to take its faithful stand
Before the Holy of Holies where the high God
Spoke in spirit form to special prophets.

76 . Almandine is 'an alumina iron garnet of a violet or amethystine tint' (*Shorter Oxford English Dictionary*). Peridot is a kind of chrysolite. Pynkardine is unknown. Possibly cornelian.

77 . Gollancz (op. cit., vol. 1, p. xxviii) thinks 'the magic birds of Gathonolabes, who dwelt in the land of Prester John, may have suggested the birds on the branches of the golden candlesticks'.

78 . 'It', i.e. the great candelabrum mentioned in l. 1478, and earlier, l. 1272.

The Wielder of all under the welkin, you may well believe,
Hated that orgy, the hideous circumstance
That japers should foully juggle with his jewels so noble
Which had proved so precious in his presence formerly.

In his sacrifices some had been solemnly anointed
Through the summons he himself made, sitting on high.
Now a braggart on a bench boozed from them
Till drunk as the devil, he drivelled where he sat.

So the Creator of the earth was utterly outraged,
And as their revel ran riot, he pre-arranged his purpose,
Ascertaining he would not harm them with hasty anger,
By warning them in a weird and wonderful way.

Now the treasures were to be taken for the tippling of
  gluttons,
Set up in royal state and sumptuously polished.
Belshazzar boldly bid people drink from them:
'Swill the wine here, wassail!' he cried.[79]

Then swift servants speedily ran up
And caught cups in their hands that the kings might be
  served.
In the bright bowls others blithely poured wine,
And each man ministered to his master only.

When the castle servants caught up the cups in their hands,
The rich metal rang resonantly in truth,
And the clattering of cup-covers as the concubines threw
  them off
Sang as sweetly sounding as a sonnet on a psaltery.

79. 'Wassail' = *wes hal* = 'health be to you' (Anglo-Saxon).

That dolt on the dais gulped down the lot;
Then drink was set down for the dukes and princes,
The concubines and courteous knights, in the cause of
   pleasure;
Each drank to the dregs the drink that was brought him.[80]

The lords delighted long in the liquor so sweet,
Glorying in their false gods, grovelling to them for grace,
Who were but stocks and stones, stationary for ever,
Never a sound slipping out, so still were their tongues –

All the golden gods the Gauls still call on,
Baal-peor and Belial, and Beelzebub as well,[81]
They hailed them as holily as if they owned heaven;
But him who grants all good, that God they forgot.

The Writing on the Wall

A marvellous miracle happened, which many men saw:
It came to the king first, and all the court afterwards.
In that princely palace, on a plain wall,
Close by where the candelabrum most clearly shone,

There appeared a spirit hand with pen between fingers,
A great ghostly hand, which grimly wrote:
No other form but a fist, not fastened to a wrist,
Was penning on the plaster, portraying letters.

80. The wassail ceremony required that the drinker finish his
drink at a single draught.

81. In Numbers xxv, 3, Baal-peor (roughly, Lord of Self-
glorification) was a god to whom the Israelites turned in one of
their idolatrous periods. Beelzebub (= 'Lord of the Flies') was to
the Jews the chief of false gods. 'Belial' is Hebrew for 'devil'.

When bold Belshazzar looked at that bunched-up fist,
Such a dazing dread drenched his heart
That he blanched livid and lost his composure.
The strength of the stroke strained his joints,

His knees were clenched close, he collapsed sagging;
Then hitting with his hands, he hurt his own face,
And bawled like a bull bellowing in terror,
His eyes ever on the hand till all was written,
Where it rasped on the rough wall its runic saying.

When it had scraped the scripture with its scribe's pen,
As a coulter carves the clay in furrows,
In verity it vanished, avoiding their sight;
But the letters were left, written large in the plaster.

When the king was so recovered that he could speak again,
He instructed his scholars to study it close at hand
And explain what was penned, what its purpose was,
'For it frightens my flesh, with its fingers so grim.'

The scholars studied it to seek its meaning.
But the wisest was not aware what one word meant,
Or what lore or language its letters belonged to,
Or what tale or tidings was betokened by the signs.

Then bold Belshazzar nearly became mad,
Sending out searchers the whole city round
For men wise in witchcraft, or warlocks perhaps,
Who dealt in demonology and could decipher dark letter-
   ing.

'Call them all to my court, those Chaldean clerks;
Tell them the truth of this terrible happening,

And clamorously proclaim: "The clerk who can tell the
    king,
Explaining in speech what is spelled by those letters,

'"And satisfy my spirit with the sense expressed,
Making its meaning manifest to me,
Shall be gowned most gaily in garments of purple,
And a collar of clear gold shall be clasped at his throat;

'"He shall be primate and prince of the priesthood itself,
And of all held in honour here, he shall be third,
And the richest in the realm of those who ride with me,
The best of all but two; and be the third." '

His call was proclaimed, and there came many
Of the cleverest clerks Chaldea knew;
Sage old satraps, steeped in sorcery,[82]
And wizards and witches went to the palace,

Diviners of dreams, demonologers,
Sorcerers, spirit-charmers, and many sorts of magician.
They looked at the letters and were enlightened no more
Than if they'd looked at the leather of my left boot.

Then the king clawed his clothes and cried out in frenzy.
What! He cursed his clerks and called them slaves,
And had the hapless fools hurriedly hanged;
So wild and witless was he, he almost went mad.

The chief queen heard him cursing from her quarters above,
And when she was aware of what had caused it,
That change to ill-chance in the chief hall,

82. A satrap was a Persian provincial governor. The term was
not understood by medieval Englishmen. Our poet, like Wy-
cliffe, simply understands it as 'wise man'.

The lady, to lessen the loss of her lord,
Glided down graciously to go to the King.

On the cold stone kneeling she sank, and spoke to him
Words of wisdom, in a worshipful manner:

'Mighty king,' said the queen, 'Conqueror of the world,
Everlasting be your life in its length of days!
Why have you rent your robe in reckless dismay
Because those ignorant clerks could not decode these letters,

'When you have a man at hand, as I have often heard,
Possessed of the spirit of the all-seeing God of truth?
His soul is skilled and can solve riddles,
Open up the hidden truths of outlandish events.

'He is the one who was able to raise up your father
With holy words from the hot rage into which he often fell.
When Nebuchadnezzar was nearly distracted,
He interpreted with total truth his dreams,

'Saved him with sage counsel from a sinister fate;
All the king's questions he quickly answered perfectly
Through the power of the spirit present within him
From the most glorious gods who govern anywhere.

'For his deep divinity and judicious advice,
Your bold father, Belshazzar, bore rule by his help;
Daniel of dark knowledge men deem the man,
He who was caught and captured in the country of the Jews;

'Nebuchadnezzar took him, and now he is here,
A prophet of that province, most prominent in the world.
Send into the city to seek him quickly,
And honourably ask him to answer your questions;

'And though the sentence be obscure that is scratched there,
He will tell the truth betokened on the clay wall.'
The good counsel of the queen was caught on to at once,
And Daniel was brought to Belshazzar before very long.

When he came to the king and courteously hailed him,
Belshazzar embraced him. 'Beloved sir,' he said,
You are a true interpreter, men tell me so,
A prophet of that province plundered by my father,

'And that you have in your heart a holy magic,
A soul mysteriously foreseeing truth;
The God who governs all has given you his spirit,
And you make clear the king of heaven's arcane purposes.

'A marvel has been manifested here, and most gladly
Would I be certain of the sense of what is inscribed on the
    wall;
For all the clerks in Chaldea have most cravenly failed.
If your craft can conquer it, I shall requite you well;

'For if you read it aright, with reason in your interpretation,
First telling me the text of the entwined letters,
And then make manifest the meaning of the thought to me,
I shall hold to the oath I now offer before you:

'I shall put on you a purple robe, of perfect fine cloth,
And a band of brilliant gold about your neck,
And of those that throng after me you shall be third noblest.
A baron on the bench you shall be, no less.'

The prophet Daniel then promptly replied to him:
'Royal king of this realm, heaven's ruler protect you!
It was certainly seen that the Sovereign of heaven
Brought fortune to your father, and confirmed his power,

'Granted it him to be greatest of all governors ever,
Doing his will in the world in whatever way he liked:
Whom God wishes well, well will that man prosper;
Him whose death he desires, he destroys quickly.

'Whoever he likes to lift up, will be aloft in a moment,
Or to lay low, and low he will quickly lie.
So Nebuchadnezzar was renowned for his power,
His rule strongly established by the staunchness of God,

'For he wholly believed in the Highest in his heart,
And knew plainly that all his power from that Prince came.
As long as that belief was locked in his heart,
No mighty man on earth had as much power as he;

'Until the time came, when he was touched with pride,
His sovereignty being so spacious, so splendid his life;
For his own actions he had so huge a regard
That the power of heaven's prince he completely forgot.

'So he began to blaspheme and to blame the Lord,
And imagined his might to be as much as God's:
"I am god of the entire globe, which I govern as I please,
Like him high in heaven who rules angels.

'"If he has formed the firmament and the folk on earth,
I have built Babylon, the best and greatest city,
Established every stone there by the strength of my arms:
No might but mine may ever make such another."

'No sooner was this speech sent from his mouth
Than the saying of the Sovereign sounded in his ears:
"Now Nebuchadnezzar, enough of such words!
Now your power and principality pass from you;

'"Removed from the sons of men, on the moors you must live,
Walking the wastes and dwelling with wild animals,
Browsing on grass and bracken like a beast of the plain,
With fierce wolves and wild asses in the wilderness."

'From the pinnacle of his pride he departed then,
Left his stately seat and his solaces behind,
And was cast out full of care to countries unknown,
Far into a forest where friendly men never came.

'He was strangely obsessed, and seemed to himself
To be but a beast, a bull or an ox.
He went forth on all fours, feeding on grass,
Eating hay like a horse when the herbage was withered.

'That king of consequence counted himself a cow;
And so seven seasons, with their summers, went by.
By then, there were thick hairs thrusting from his flesh,
Which was dressed and adorned in the dew of heaven.

'Long and lank fell his loathsome hair,
Shaggy and dishevelled from shoulder to groin,
And twining twentyfold, it tumbled to his toes,
Matted and mired as if mixed with plaster.

'His beard grew over his breast to the bare earth,
His brows bristled like briars above his broad cheeks,
His eyes were hollow under hoary lashes,
And all was as grey as the great buzzard, with grim talons

'That were cruel and crooked as the claws of a kite;
Hued like an eagle he was; so hued all over.
Then his mind at last admitted the might of the Lord,
Who can cast away kingdoms, or recover them, as he pleases.

'Then his senses were restored, after his suffering and sorrow;
So that his knowledge was renewed, and he knew himself
   again.
Then he loved the Lord and believed in him truly;
He only, and no other, held all in his hand.

'Then speedily he was sent back, his throne restored,
And his state was swiftly set up once more.
Happy at his return, his earls bowed to him,
And his complexion appeared in its proper hue again.

'But you, Belshazzar, his first-born and his heir,
Observe these signs and discount them entirely.
You have ever set your heart against the high God,
Bragging and blaspheming, hurling boasts at him.

'And now with filthy vanity you have defiled his vessels,
Whose high function was to honour his house from the first;
You have dragged them before your dukes and poured drink
   in them,
Given wine to your wenches in a wicked moment.

'You have brought beverages to the board in vessels
Blessed by bishops' hands in blithe ceremony,
Giving glory to lifeless gods with your toasts,
Gods of stocks and stones unable to stir a foot.

'And for that frothing filth the Father of heaven
Has sent into this state-room this strange sight,
The fist with the fingers that flayed your heart,
With a rough pen rasping runes on the wall:

'The sentence inscribed states as follows,
Each figure, I find, as our Father framed it:
MENE, TEKEL, PERES: a three-fold phrase.
It threatens you in three ways for your thriftless folly.

148

'To expound the spell speedily, I proceed:
MENE means this much: "Almighty God
Has counted up your kingdom by clear numbers
In good faith to its farthest end, and it is finished."

'To tell of TEKEL now, the term means this:
"Your splendid sway is set on the scales in balance,
And weighed, is found wanting in worthy deeds."
And PERES follows for those faults, to affirm truly.

'I find in PERES in faith these fearful words:
"Your state shall be sundered, dispossessed shall you be;
Your governorship shall go from you and be given to the
     Persians;
The Medes shall be masters here, and your might thrown
     out."'

The king at once commanded them to clothe the wise man
In garments of gay cloth, as his agreement required.
Then was Daniel dressed in the dearest purple,
And a collar of clear gold clasped about his neck.

A decree was proclaimed by the king himself:
At Belshazzar's bidding he must be obeyed
By all the common people of Chaldea whom the king ruled,
As to a precious prince approved as the third,

The highest of all others save only two,
Servant of Belshazzar in city and field.
This was quickly proclaimed at court and made known,
And the liegemen of the lord were delighted by it.

But however Daniel was dealt with, that day passed,
And now night neared with numberless troubles;
For that dark being done, not one day dawned
Before the doom was dealt that Daniel had foreseen.

The splendid festivity in that solemn hall
Did not cease till the sun began to set,
And the blue of bright heaven became paler;
The mild day turned murky and the mists drove

Along the low meadows under the lowering sky.
Each man hurried to his own house then,
Sat at his supper and sang afterwards;
And clusters of guests were leaving till late in the night.

Belshazzar was borne to his bed in bliss,
Got his right rest, and never rose again.
For his foes had flocked to the field in hosts:
They had long sought to destroy the state of that prince,

And had all assembled suddenly at the same time.
Yet they had no inkling of it all in the palace.
There was the doughty Darius, duke of the Medes,
The proud prince of Persia, Porus of India,[83]

A multitude of men, many huge legions,
Who had picked the perfect moment to plunder Chaldea.
They thronged in the darkness there, thickly pressing for-
    ward,
Skimmed over the sparkling waters and scaled the walls,

Drew forward long ladders and lifted them up,
And stole silently into the city, with no stir made.
Within the first hour of the night their entry was effected
And no defender woke in fear; further they went,

83. Porus gets into the story from the alliterative *Wars of
Alexander.*

And approached the principal palace in silence.
Then they ran forward in a rout, rushing in thousands.
Blasts from bright bugles burst forth aloud:
The shouts were heaven-shaking; men shivered with terror.

Sleepers were slain before they could escape,
And every place was pillaged and plundered in a flash.
Belshazzar was battered to death in his bed,
His blood and his brains blending with the sheets.

Then the king was caught up in his curtain by the heels,
Dragged forth by the feet and foully abused –
He who that day had so daringly drunk from the vessels.
Now a dog lying in a ditch is more dignified than he.

For in the morning the master of the Medes arose;
Doughty Darius, placed that day on the throne,
Seized a fully sound city, and established peace
With all the barons thereabout, who bowed to his rule.

Thus was that land lost through the lord's sin
And his filthy foulness when defilement was thrown
On the ornaments of God's house that had been holily
   blessed.
He was accursed for his uncleanness and caught by it,

Dragged down from his dignity for his dreadful deeds,
Cast out for ever from the honoured of this world:
And most probably deprived of pleasures above, too –
His looking on our lovely Lord would be long deferred!

Thus in three ways I have thoroughly shown you
That uncleanness is cleft asunder in the courteous heart
Of our gracious God who governs heaven,
Arousing him to wrath, raising his vengeance.

But cleanness is his comfort, and courtesy he loves,
And the seemly and sweet ones shall see his face.
May we go in gay garments and be granted grace,
That we may serve in his sight where solace never ceases!

AMEN

THE OWL AND THE
NIGHTINGALE

INTRODUCTION

'THE OWL AND THE NIGHTINGALE is an early med-ieval English poem, which was probably written about one hundred and sixty years before Chaucer was in his prime as a poet. It is a debate between two birds, each of whom allegorically represents a system of values of the kind trad-itionally associated with her. Part of the achievement of this extraordinary poem lies in the fact that the values discussed in it, sophisticated and humane as they are, are presented in concrete popular language without a trace of poetic diction or intellectual persiflage. The two birds are birds from the world of popular fable, whose slanging match – for that is what it turns out to be, until their closing agreement to seek an external examiner to pronounce on their debate – is con-ducted in domestic and rural terms, precise, vivid and often so direct that one translator (J. W. H. Atkins, 1922) resorts to rows of dots rather than bowdlerize the occasional robust obscenities. The style is colloquial, and the debate lasts for a time appropriate to these particular birds: from early evening until the early morning, when in their dawn chorus birds such as the thrush and the blackbird (1.1658), and, a little later, the Wren (1.1718), come to support the Night-ingale. The debate is conducted according to the rules of ecclesiastical rather than civil law; '. . . the legal vocabulary is almost entirely English, many of the technical legal terms being derived from the pre-Conquest legal vocabulary'.[1] But a comic rider lights every stage of the contest: has the particular charge, defence or abusive attack been conducted in such a way as to make the opponent lose her temper, and

1. R. M. Wilson, *Early Middle English Literature* (Methuen, 1939), p. 167.

so become unfit to continue pleading? At the conclusion of almost every speech the poet amusingly describes the opponent's effort to master her anger and confusion, which are manifested Owl-wise or Nightingale-wise, according to the lore attached to the particular bird.

In the course of the debate each bird comprehensively defines her own position and presses her attack on her rival as far as words will take it; and then they fly off together to submit their case to judgement. The poem ends before the judge appears, so that the listener is left to make his own judgement; or, if he finds something persuasive in both sets of argument, to effect his own synthesis. The poem is thus a work of high civilization, the implicit intention of the poet being to express, in the form of a literary debate, a complex interpretation of important contemporary ideas. These are approached ostensibly through the contest between Nightingale-song and Owl-song, which appear to stand for, respectively, the ideas of courtly love poetry and the traditional morals and faith recommended by the Church. But we find as we proceed that, although the climax of the debate is concerned with love and marriage more than anything else, a whole philosophy of life emerges from the conflict, a charitable, pragmatic and – yes – humanistic system of values superior to that inherent in either of the formal positions taken up by the two birds. The persuasive power of the poet, rather than that of either of the birds, is such as to constitute an invitation to continue the debate after his performance has ended. He displays several different oratorical and poetic styles, and makes his protagonists advance their sophisticated arguments with illustrations drawn from a rich background of learned and popular lore; besides which, he vividly characterizes his two birds, and writes entertainingly with alternate humour and earnestness.

The appearance of an English poem of such refinement

little more than a hundred years after the Norman Conquest perhaps needs explaining, since it was written about two hundred years before the native language superseded Latin as the recognized vehicle for literature, and since we are generally taught that English artistic culture and language were in an unformed state during the twelfth century, owing to the dissolving interaction of Norman French and native English in all matters of government, religion and learning. But that is not quite accurate; England's part in the primitive Renaissance of the twelfth century was like that of an almost destitute mother welcoming home a growing and prosperous child. Until the second half of the ninth century early Christian Ireland had been the chief home of Western learning for about two hundred years; and a noble and soon virtually independent offshoot of Irish learning had developed in the north of England, culminating in the achievements of Bede (673–735) and his school. Then with the arrival of the Danes, and such disasters as their destruction in 867 of the finest library in the Western world, which was at York, a decline set in. But across the Channel the revival of letters initiated by Charlemagne, who drew to his court scholars from Ireland, Spain and Italy, was guided by the Englishman Alcuin, a disciple of Bede. Thus there is a strong connection, through teaching, learning and writing over the generations, between Bede and Alcuin of the eighth century and Abelard and Bernard of Chartres of the twelfth. John of Salisbury, a contemporary of our poet, who studied at Chartres and Paris, and came under the influence of Abelard, became the friend and secretary of Becket, and may be called the founder of Renaissance learning in England. Through him, and through people like Walter Map the satirist and William of Malmesbury the chronicler, a genuine sense of classical learning, partly freed from the pedantry and doctrinal rigidity of the Church, came into England.

The tradition represented by Bede had taken from classical learning chiefly its rhetorical techniques and linguistic training, which it had then applied to the Bible and other devotional writings. But the feeling for the classical world which showed itself positively in the twelfth century was different. It was concerned with the material of the literature, with the literature as literature, and with the civilization reflected in it. One characteristic of pagan poetry had been its comprehensive delineation of love; passionate, idealistic, cynical, obscene. And with this quality in particular the Christian church conducted a kind of love–hate relationship. On the one hand was the beautiful Latin language, the international devotional tongue used in Jerome's Bible; on the other, in the linguistic models which had to be studied if clerics were to develop erudition and the high style, were values deeply repugnant to ascetic monotheism. The result was that, in spite of periodical episcopal fulminations against pagan poetry (Cistercians were actually forbidden to write rhyming poetry at all by the end of the twelfth century[2]), a body of fine secular poetry in Latin was created in and around the medieval cloister, much of it on the subject of profane love. Thus it was that, before the Church more powerfully asserted its defensive orthodoxy in the thirteenth century, the excitement of the new movement penetrated widely. And beside it, as a kind of complement to it, though its origins were diverse, came the new Romance culture of poetry and music, and the inflammatory heretical doctrine of courtly love.

Against this background the appearance of 'The Owl and The Nightingale', which exhibits the assured use of a Romance metre and of a literary convention handed down from antiquity, is not so surprising. The poem is the first of

2. Helen Waddell, *The Wandering Scholars* (Constable, 7th ed. revised, 1934), p. 102.

substantial length and merit to be written in English in octosyllabic couplets, which lend themselves particularly well to epigrammatic statement, especially of lightly emphasized apophthegms, and to racy narration, knockabout humour and downright abuse. They also remained a regular metre for lyric and pastoral elegy until the seventeenth century. Provided the poet could manage his rhymes, and use the iambic tetrameter flexibly and musically, he might find it a better instrument for his purposes than other metres available. One of these was English alliterative verse, which is fine for epic narrative but tends to heaviness, and the other was Romance stanzaic verse, all varieties of which tend, with their built-in invitation to the poet to supply regular units of sense, to interrupt the flow of narrative or argument.

The *débat* (the French word concentrates attention on the literary form) became a characteristically medieval form of the contest of wit found in Latin pastoral poetry. In Theocritus and Virgil, for instance, there are contests between shepherds, often involving singing. The opening narrative usually includes a description of a pastoral setting and a definition of the nature of the contest, and the conclusion of the poem is the judgement, as in Virgil's seventh eclogue. The medieval modification was to shift the emphasis from the contestant's skill in singing or argument to the validity of the ideas they presented or represented: a shift from the personal to the general, or from the technical and particular to the moral and universal. In the twelfth and thirteenth centuries, the debate came to be the vehicle for the examination of all sorts of themes and antitheses – such as body and soul, sun and moon, gold and lead, winter and summer, wine and water, and, not surprisingly in view of the literary preoccupations of the age, Phyllis and Flora, which considered the respective merits of knights and clerics as lovers. The contestants were usually allegorical figures which represented rival sets of values. In religious debate the method, which was practised by Abelard, was, as in 'The Owl and the Nightingale', deliberately not to provide a conclusion, but to 'encourage beginners to search for the truth; secondly, to put them in a position to acquire truth for themselves, and thus to sharpen their wits as a result of their search' (Atkins, 'The Owl and the Nightingale', p.xlviii). Atkins (op.cit., p.lvi) regards the poem as a conflict between religious didactic poetry and secular love poetry rather than between the values associated with each; but whichever emphasis is preferred, literary forms and literary values are both involved.

This concentration on moral specifications derived from the medieval church, which was coming into its full heritage in a more or less settled Europe. In the new atmosphere of confidence the vernacular had to be recognized as a respectable means of literary communication to stand beside the language of learned Europe, Latin. Most kings and nobles did not know Latin: 'Rex illiteratus asinus coronatus' (an illiterate king is a crowned donkey). But whether they knew Latin or not, whether or not indeed they could read at all – and Henry II, the king surely mentioned in line 1079, was about the most learned monarch in the Europe of his day – they could be approached through their ears with polite and religious literature. So courtly poetry in the vernacular, already strong in commemorative epic, romance and love-song, was reinforced by didactic literature inspired by the Church, in which category 'The Owl and the Nightingale' is the best early English poem.

The reasonable assumption that the poem was written for a particular cultivated circle has led to attempts to read into it precise political, as well as moral and religious, allegory. J. C. Russell[3] thinks it may have been written by a canon

3. 'The Patrons of The Owl and the Nightingale', Philological Quarterly, vol. 47, April 1969, No. 2, pp. 178–85.

lawyer and professor called Nicholas, the main seat of whose family was near Guildford, for an Oxford occasion at which his patron Geoffrey was present. Geoffrey was the illegitimate son of Henry II who was Archbishop of York from 1189 to 1212, a somewhat cantankerous but virtuous man whom Russell sees as the Owl of the poem. His Nightingale is Richard I (1189–99), whose life-style as crusader and song-writer fitted him for the role. Anne H. Baldwin[4] sees the poem as a satire on Henry II, in which the values of the Nightingale are not unjustifiably attached to the learned king who husbanded perhaps the most famous of the queens of courtly love, Eleanor of Aquitaine. The Owl, whom Miss Baldwin considers the victor in the debate, is Thomas à Becket, the Archbishop of Canterbury whose long quarrel with the king ended in martyrdom in his own cathedral, an event which in turn provided medieval England with its most popular saint. If she is right, sharp point is given to some of the matter in the poem. Marie de France's 'Lay of the Austic', which is referred to by the Owl and commented on by the Nightingale (ll. 1049–1101), contains two incidents which resemble well-known episodes from Henry's life. One was that he put his queen under lock and key for conspiring against him with her sons, and the other was that he caught her in *flagrante delicto* with Raoul de Faye. Significantly, the Owl later justifies adultery by the wife of a bad husband (ll. 1539–70). In Anne Baldwin's interpretation the Owl becomes, like Becket, a Christ-figure. It is true that the implication of lines 1607–30 is virtually unavoidable, given the medieval penchant for drawing parallels; and if the Owl's attitude to adultery is thought to be too latitudinarian for Christ, a check on the way Jesus handled the case of the woman taken in adultery (John viii, 1–11) will be found re-

4. 'Henry II and *The Owl and the Nightingale*', *Journal of English and German Philology*, vol. 66, 1967, pp. 207–29.

assuring. All the same, the fact that the Owl seems to repre-sent herself as Christ-like on this one occasion during the debate does not mean that the poet thinks of her in the same way throughout. The generally light and humorous tone of the poem, and the frequency with which the Owl in particu-lar is made to look absurd, surely persuade the reader to be as detached from both the protagonists as the poet is from all his material.

The detachment and apparent light-heartedness of the poet might have led to his not being taken seriously, but I think they were wisely circumspect; he was working in a new field, contrasting in literary allegory a new way of thinking, that of courtly love poetry, with a whole spectrum of religious thinking. Such heterodoxies as either of his birds might be likely to utter would be more safely spoken through their beaks in native English, and not by his own (no doubt priestly) mouth in the language which might take it to the guardians of religious orthodoxy all over Europe.

Stanley (op.cit., p.22) thought that 'the argument is far from neat,' but J. W. H. Atkins, who edited and made a literal translation of the poem in 1922, regarded it as in some ways the first piece of English literary criticism and refers to its 'well-designed structure'.[5] Some indication of the way the argument is found to work may help the reader to discover the strength or weakness of the poet's design, and its relation to his material; and to judge whether he does offer 'serious answers to the serious questions' he raises.

The technique of the poet is to use a kind of chain-stitch to link the stages of the argument. A major charge laid by one of the contestants will often have been mentioned, though in slightly different form, at an earlier stage of the debate, as a piece of incidental abuse; and it may be mentioned later in

5. *English Literary Criticism: The Medieval Phase*, (Methuen, 1943) p. 143.

the debate, again in a slightly altered form. Then, a piece of incidental abuse may not be answered immediately by the listening bird, but may be rebutted, again incidentally, in a later reply to a quite different charge of substance. These are the poet's deliberate means of binding consecutive elements in the conflict and so helping the listener to keep all the subject matter in focus at any stage of the debate. Then, as I also hope to demonstrate, he lavishes his best arguments, debating style and sympathy on each bird in turn. The sympathy is always appropriate to the object: no languishing lyricism is wasted on the Owl, nor earnest and sober commendation on the Nightingale. A summary commentary on the debate will best show what I mean.

Lines 1–214. The argument begins with everything apparently loaded heavily against the Owl. While the Nightingale's setting is full of beauty and burgeoning, the Owl's is ugly and barren; yet there is a glimmer of hope for the Owl, for the decayed stump on which she sits is overgrown with ivy, which in Christian symbolism represents everlasting life, being evergreen. The clue to the validity of the Owl's system of values has thus been laid as early as line 26. Yet already the poet has made a preliminary declaration in favour of the Nightingale, *in propria persona*, by praising her song and saying

> Indeed all men declare with right
> That she [the Owl]'s a hideous, loathsome sight.   (31–2)

The poet continues to show the Owl in an unfavourable light by making her threaten the Nightingale with violence (which a medieval audience, accustomed to the techniques of allegory, would take simply to represent the Church's hostility to the tenets of courtly love). This leads to the Nightingale's long condemnation of the Owl's ugliness, foul habits and failure to transcend her abominable natural origins

163

(ll. 56–138). So far the argument has mostly concerned aesthetics (which bird looks or sounds the more *beautiful*), but in the hawk fable (ll. 101–38) the moral element enters with discussion of nurture; the kind of nurture being dependent on the place in the chain of being held by the creature under discussion. The Owl, not being a hawk (though she later claims kinship with both hawk and eagle), is bound to have degraded habits. It is fundamentally a Platonic argument.

The poet finds the Owl's discomfiture funny:

> [She] sat as swollen on her log
> As if she'd gobbled up a frog –   (145–6)

and in this propensity to make fun of the Owl much more than of the Nightingale, irrespective of the weight he gives to their respective arguments, I see a certain sign that the poem was written for a courtly audience. The odiousness of the Owl has to be established at the outset, to ensure that the audience, presumably being devotees of the Nightingale, will go on listening, secure in their mistaken feeling that they are not going to receive a sermon. Thus the Owl repeats her threat of violence by issuing a physical challenge to the much smaller Nightingale. The latter merely scoffs at the Owl for her treachery, and the first point of rest comes with the agreement of the two birds to submit their case to Nicholas of Guildford, in whom each bird trusts, recognizing in him her own qualities. The terms in which they represent him are important: the Nightingale connects his virtue with his judgement in music, whereas the Owl respects his impartiality because he has left the pleasures of youth behind. Round One to the Nightingale.

Lines 215–548. The 'second round' starts with a repetition of the Nightingale's charge, but this time the aesthetic complaint about the Owl's song is supported by the moral complaint that the Owl is a thing of darkness, blind by day, and therefore evil. The Owl, in her first reply of substance, establishes her dignity in the face of vexatious little birds, and claims to act in harmony with her own nature. She also asserts her priestly function in signalling the hours of prayer during the night (ll. 323–8). Her regulated night-song, she says, obeys the divinely sanctioned principle of moderation, while the Nightingale, in contrast, sings undiscriminatingly all night long. The argument is both moral and aesthetic. She meets the Nightingale's charge that she is blind by day with a flat denial, and claims that her night-vision is especially useful when she is fulfilling the function of the hawk in accompanying warriors at night.

In her reply the Nightingale for the first time links the song of the Owl with adversity, and assumes the Owl's envy of happiness:

> When joy and bliss spread wide and free
> You're eaten up by jealousy.
> You're like the man of evil spite
> To whom all joy's a loathsome sight. (419–22)

The Nightingale answers the charge that her singing is indiscriminate by pointing out that she sings only in spring, 'though never going on too long', but then lays herself open to a fresh charge by declaring 'winter's ruin is not for me' (l. 458). That ivy is going to be important.

The Owl rejoices in her winter function of being host to man (l. 475–80) and celebrating Christmas, and accuses the Nightingale afresh of immoderation in egging on the licentiousness of spring and summer, and of actually personifying both post-coital lassitude and the impermanence of love based on sexual impulses alone. The Owl has now built up a formidable position based on her moderation, her gifts of strength and comfort in adversity, and her devout utility.

The Nightingale attempts to return to the charge, but the Owl rightly claims that it is her turn to attack. Round Two to the Owl.

Lines 549–892. The single skill. As the Owl lets fly with her new charge, which is that the Nightingale possesses no good attribute except her voice, she incidentally launches three minor counter-charges which balance attacks made on herself earlier. The first is that the Nightingale is ugly, and therefore (Platonic doctrine again) lacking in virtue:

> Beauty somehow passed you by;
> Your virtue, too, 's in short supply. (581–2)

The second is that she lives by the privy, and the third that she eats dirty food. The Owl incidentally rebuts the Nightingale's earlier charge that her habits are filthy by pointing out that all babies, even human ones, foul their immediate surroundings. The Owl's description of her lair at this point (ll. 617–20) is an important reminder that she stands for evergreen eternity.

The Nightingale's long reply to the charge that she possesses only one skill (ll. 707–836) constitutes a recommendation that quality is to be preferred to quantity; the sympathy this evokes in the audience is strengthened by the Nightingale's special claim (ll. 715–42) to represent the joyous aspect of Christian worship, that aspect which blissfully celebrates the eternal life to come. Stanley[6] notes the contemporary concern whether the new, joyous, style of worship, of the kind to be associated with St Francis in the next few years, was to be preferred to 'the older devotional approach ... through weeping lamentation, mindful that this world is a vale of tears, where death comes in the end to sinful man'.

6. op. cit., p. 24.

As the latter is described by the Owl (ll. 856-92), it makes a less inviting appeal. Round Three to the Nightingale, but only just; because, by not once mentioning love in defence of her 'one skill', she has hypocritically deceived the courtly audience into feeling good about the association of nightingale song with Christian worship. She wins the round by debating skill rather than by the moral or aesthetic value of what she says.

Lines 893-1042

> My song helps virtuous men to yearn;
> I sing when they with longing burn   (889-90)

is logically the end of the third round, although it comes in the middle of a long speech by the Owl; because the graver bird now brings up as a substantive charge an indictment previously made incidentally, but with power, when she was defending herself (ll. 488-522). Then, she made great fun of post-coital lassitude at the Nightingale's expense; a limited, physical matter, except for the associated charge that sexual love is brief. Now (ll. 893-932), this idea is extended in an attack on the Nightingale's claim to represent the essence of Christian worship (ll. 715-42). The Owl asserts that song which lures to love is irrelevant to the spread of the faith, in which the Nightingale is clearly not interested, since she does not sing in northern parts, where missionary work is urgently needed (ll. 903-7). The Nightingale's reply (ll. 995-1042), that northerners are savage and unredeemable, is thoroughly irresponsible, and complements her earlier expressed distaste for winter. It now looks as if, seeing that Round Four goes to the Owl, the Nightingale is going to lose the battle.

Lines 1043-1290. But the Owl now overplays her hand: her delight in the torture inflicted on the guilty nightingale of the courtly love stories alienates sympathy, and the Nightingale seizes the chance to demonstrate not only that the jealous lord was punished and shamed, but that she has the sympathy of all mankind, which derives from her compassion for lovers and her happy attitude, while the Owl is universally abhorred. Nevertheless, by admitting that 'the first good use can then be got' (l. 1122) of the Owl when she is used as a scarecrow, she provides the opportunity, which the Owl eventually takes in her peroration (ll. 1603–34), for the Owl to claim a Christ-like function. Meanwhile, however, the role of the Owl in foreseeing disasters is the subject of the Nightingale's fresh charge (ll. 1149–74). Here the poet nicely balances frankly human predilections: while the listener reacts emotionally in favour of, and intellectually against, the Nightingale's desire to look only on the pleasant side of life:

> Cursed be the beadle with his shout
> Who spreads such wretched truths about!
> Who always brings unpleasant news
> And burdens men with loathsome views! (1169–71)

he reacts insidiously against the Owl's claim to remain above the conflict in a superhuman way – a claim she substantiates from a traditional standpoint concerned with justice and retribution rather than from one dominated by compassion for suffering humanity. I award the round to the Nightingale.

Lines 1291–1602. The last 'round' of the debate is the most important, as it is the one after which the appeal to judgement is made; and it is accordingly the one upon which closest evaluation of the author's purposes can be based. It is quite remarkable to a twentieth-century reader that when two apparently medieval temperaments as naturally opposed as those of the Owl and the Nightingale discuss love, marriage

and adultery, they should for the first time seem to be in harmony, through the expression of latitudinarian, common-
sense, compassionate views of a pragmatic and almost
modern kind. Yet their opinions are developed with different and complementary emphases, and their hostility to each
other is maintained with all the fury of the old dialectical
charade. The last flourish of this is the Owl's claim to be still
of service to Man after death, as a scarecrow, and the Nightingale's counter-claim that that very assertion, being utterly
shameful, must lose the Owl the battle:

> In boasting of your own disgrace,
> You grant to me the winner's place.   (1651–2)

After that, the return to the initial position of the *débat*, one of
physical menace, is formal, a kind of punctuation at the end
of the argument, which acts incidentally to evoke the inter-
cessory appearance of the Wren, the King of the Birds,[7] who
has to protect both from the human condemnation they
would receive if they started a war.

The curious way in which human and avian values are
related is of the essence of fable. Classical beast-fable, as
represented by Aesop, presented common wisdom rather
than religious teaching; but when medieval theological
writers commented on classical fables, or invented new ones,
they applied to them the techniques of devout allegorizing.
The effect of this was to make the fictitious beast-world sub-
servient to the human world, so that, however edifying the

7. The Wren became King of the Birds in the following way.
It was agreed by the birds that their king should be the bird which
flew highest. The Eagle could naturally fly higher than the rest,
but when he was at the highest point of his flight, the Wren, who
had taken a ride thus high under the Eagle's wing, climbed out on
top.

morals that might be drawn, the actual beast-world envis-
aged was devitalized.[8] Throughout medieval beast-fable
there is a corrupting attitude of condescension to the beast-
world; and it shows in 'The Owl and the Nightingale' in
the writer's attitude to the Wren:

> She was considered wise, the Wren,
> Having been reared in realms of men.
> From them she'd got her canny head:
> She was not in the woodlands bred.   (1723–6)

However, the aim of the medieval beast-fable is fundamentally a religious one, the loftiness of which carries its own justification. Isidore of Seville called fable 'a fiction in which,
through the conversation of dumb animals, an image of life
is presented;'[9] the 'life' he was concerned with being, of
course, exclusively human and Christian.

Three of the main subjects debated must now be discussed
in more detail. The first of these has to do with religious attitudes, in which the Owl is given the traditional strength and
inflexibility of orthodoxy, while the Nightingale, insofar as
her declarations can be accepted at face value, tends to the
kind of ecstatic worship which was a counterpart to the
mood of the secular adorings of courtly love. Two aspects of
the Owl's position stand out. One is her winter strength,
which enables her to accompany man in adversity, consoling
and fortifying, and the other is her advocacy of missionary
activities in the cold north, where as yet the Christian writ is
tenuous, or does not even run. Although, as I indicate in my

8. In just the same way, the Old Testament was devitalized at
the expense of the New. Allegorization was one way in which
Christians could reconcile the teaching of the Old Testament
with the vision and morals of the New.

9. Atkins, op. cit., p. 33.

INTRODUCTION

note to line 1016, the Church was constantly trying to extend
its sway northwards, and there are at least two, and possibly
three, missionary candidates for the compliment offered by
the poet, the reference to barbarism in the untamed north must
be considered more widely. The Nightingale (ll. 997–1042)
is expressing three kinds of contempt: that of civilization for
barbarism, that of the Romance world for the Norse world,
and that of Christian sanity for pagan unreason. But behind
the Nightingale's feverish scoffing lies terror of the savage-
dominated, monster-haunted wilderness: the Owl, like
Cardinal Vivian and Nicholas Breakspear, is prepared to
face it. The Nightingale's

> For winter's ruin is not for me (458)

parallels her failure to sympathize with untrained infants,
which contrasts strongly with the Owl's instinctive protec-
tion of the defenceless and the afflicted. The listener can surely be in no doubt as to which religious attitude the poet
recommends.

There is, however, an aspect of that attitude of the Owl
which the poet would like to modify. This appears in the
part of the debate which the Owl ought to dominate with
success, that relating to fortune and providence, the bearing
of adversity and the resort to astrology. Perhaps the poet
thought that there was something unpleasant in the Church's
acceptance of hardship on earth – something almost mercen-
ary in the idea of winning souls for a happy hereafter by
stressing that hardship. The Owl's over-confidence is expressed as early as lines 529–30:

> Adversity throws up the one
> By whom the task of worth is done.

The thought is morally unexceptionable, but for ordinary
humility's sake, should never be in the mouth of the 'one'

defined; and the Nightingale merely expresses the common human reaction when the main debate on the subject is joined (ll. 1147–1330):

> All that you sing of, soon or late,
> Is men's misfortunes, which they hate.   (1149–50)

There are two catalogues of the kinds of disorder foreseen by the Owl, one given by the Nightingale (ll. 1153–64), and the other by the Owl herself (ll. 1191–1206). Both describe disasters of the kind associated with the astrological domination of Mars and Saturn, which are marvellously evoked in two famous passages in Chaucer's 'Knight's Tale'. One of these forms part of the description of the temple of Mars:[10]

> Ther saugh I first the derke ymaginyng
> Of Felonye, and al the compassyng;
> The crueel Ire, reed as any gleede;   (live coal)
> (pick-purse)   The pykepurs, and eek the pale Drede;   (dread)
> The smyler with the knyf under the cloke;
> (stable)   The shepne brennynge with the blake smoke;
> The tresoun of the mordrynge in the bedde;
> The open werre, with woundes al bibledde;
> (strife)   Contek, with blody knyf and sharp manace.
> (harsh noise)   Al ful of chirkyng was that sory place.

and the other, only part of which I quote, is spoken by 'pale Saturnus the colde' in the heavenly discussion of the case of Palamon and Arcite.[11]

> Myn is the drenchyng in the see so wan;
> Myn is the prison in the derke cote;
> Myn is the stranglyng and hangyng by the throte,
> The murmure and the cherles rebellyng,

10. *The Poems of Chaucer*, ed. F. N. Robinson, (Houghton Mifflin, 1933) p. 42.
11. ibid, p. 48.

The groyning, and the pryvee empoysonyng;
I do vengeance and pleyn correccioun,
Whil I dwelle in the signe of the leoun ...
My lookyng is the fader of pestilence.

The Owl justifies her concentration on adversity by a fatal-
ism derived no doubt from that gracious pessimist whose
views became part of Church orthodoxy, Boethius:

> Yes, everything that's transitory
> Shall pass, like this world's ecstasy.   (1279-80)

But when she tries to justify her foreknowledge, and her in-
action concerning impending disaster, she brings on herself
the Nightingale's charge of witchcraft. The Owl did not say
how she acquired foreknowledge, apart from 'studying
written lore' (l. 1208), which the Nightingale assumes to be
astrology. Now this was a serious charge; the early Church
had made up its mind that astrology was not permitted, but
in the twelfth century, under the influence of Ptolemy's
Tetrabiblos and Arab astronomy, discussion was renewed.
St Augustine had been against it, and now John of Salisbury utterly rejected it, because astrology necessitated taking a
fatalistic view of life and, in its essential quality of predestina-
tion, infringed God's sovereignty. But Alexander of
Neckam, also a contemporary of the poet, attempted to
reconcile the influence of the stars, the divine will, and man's
spirit of free choice. It is clear from this part of the debate that
the Nightingale represents the traditional attitude of the
Church, the one which was to triumph, while the Owl
stands for Christianized astrology.[12] Her apparent complac-
ency about her power gives further credence to the Nightin-

12. See A. C. Cawley: 'Astrology in *The Owl and The
Nightingale*', *Modern Language Review*, vol. 46, April 1962, pp.
161-74, to which I am indebted here.

gale's charge of spiritual pride, which emerges over the Owl's supposed censoriousness in sexual matters (l. 1398).

By giving the Owl her particular role in the debate on fortune and foreknowledge, the poet is following a long tradition containing both learned and popular elements. The Owl was the bird of Athens, and the symbol of Pallas Athena herself, goddess of wisdom and patroness of the arts; a classical background which merged with northern traditions in the Middle Ages to produce the idea of the boding owl, the creature of the darkness shrouding the unknown. The medieval Bestiary-writer says: 'It cannot see by day, because its sight is weakened by the splendour of the rising sun.'[13] This makes it easy for him to allegorize the Owl into the Jewish nation which, of course, preferring darkness, does not recognize Jesus as the light of the world.

The last and most important subject of the debate concerns love and marriage. All through the poem there have been references preparing us for the final confrontation between the Owl and the Nightingale, every one of which reminds us of the consuming interest and violent passions aroused by consideration of the way the species maintains itself. We have to see the culmination of the debate not simply in the context of courtly love and its impact on the medieval world and religion, but in relation to preceding systems of thought which might have affected the society in which the poet lived, however remotely. We must also see those systems of thought not merely as bodying forth the religious requirements of the One Way, but as reflecting primitive survival needs of race, tribe and family group. Unproductive spilling of human seed, mating and thus propagating without guarantee of means of survival, mating outside the pair-bond, and sexual interference with either partner of a pair-bond, are

13. T. H. White, *The Book of Beasts* (Cape, 1954), p. 133.

all anti-social activities which may lead to disorder and threaten harmonious perpetuation of the species. And so they must be resisted with religious sanction. There are thus basic social reasons why the sexual activities of men and women come within the purview of religion; reasons which underlie the nature of, and help to shape, the moral and spiritual development of man.

It is beyond the scope of this essay to do more than refer briefly to the part played by asceticism, and especially sexual self-denial, in the evolution of orthodox Christianity in its first twelve hundred years. It is enough to remind readers that the founder of the religion said little enough about sex, but in that little appears, in the Sermon on the Mount (Matthew v, 28): 'But I say unto you, that whosoever looketh on a woman to lust after her hath committed adultery with her already in his heart.' Paul cast a shadow on marital love by saying: 'It is better to marry than burn' (I Corinthians vii, 9); and Origen castrated himself in the cause of his religion, following Jesus's words (Matthew xix, 12): '... and there be eunuchs, which have made themselves eunuchs for the kingdom of heaven's sake. He that is able to receive it, let him receive it.'

Small wonder then that courtly love, which exalted the sexual act outside marriage, and claimed spiritual enlightenment for its devotees, was resisted by the medieval Church with quite terrible fury. But adversaries in a conflict often influence each other; and one significant doctrinal development in that triumphant century of the Church, the twelfth, may owe something to the existence of a secular doctrine of love. This was the institution of marriage as one of the seven divinely ordained sacraments. The poet of 'The Owl and the Nightingale' reflects the finer aspects of the conflict when he looks with reason, detachment and compassion on this area of human relationship, and makes his two birds speak both lyrically and humanely about it.

The first reference to love in the poem is in the discussion about the qualities of Nicholas of Guildford, the proposed judge of the dispute. In him the medieval conflict between the rose of the world and the rose of God has been resolved, if we are to believe the Owl, by the passing of the years, which is both a universal solution and a typically medieval one. Guillaume IX of Aquitaine, a royal Provençal poet of the twelfth century, thus declares the process of the age:[14]

> Since now I have a mind to sing,
> I'll make a song of that which saddens me,
> That no more in Poitou or Limousin
> Shall I love's servant be.
>
> Of prowess and joy I had my part,
> But now of them my heart hath ta'en surcease.
> And now I go away to find that One
> Beside whom every sinner findeth peace.

In that first minor skirmish about love (ll. 189–214) the two birds take up their formal positions. Then, during those parts of the poem concerned with bird-song, religious attitudes, fortune and providence, they make a series of references to love and marriage which are mainly incidental at the time, but which prepare for, and amplify, the conclusive, central statements by the Nightingale (ll. 1331–1510) and the Owl (ll. 1511–1602). Each of these statements bears signs of having been modified in the light of the other bird's earlier contribution to the debate; I instance the Nightingale's convincing genuflexion to the conventional social functions of marriage, and the Owl's compassionate bending of the rigid frontiers of sexual sin as determined by the Church.

14. Helen Waddell's translation, op. cit., p. 127.

The Nightingale treats love as a matter of aspiration and beauty. It takes its origin from the spring, gives pleasure, and when it is manifest in the highest degree, it is an aristocratic and aesthetic experience which is justified merely by the fact that it exists between knight and lady. This courtly love had found its formal codification during the 1170s at the court of Eleanor of Aquitaine, only a short time before 'The Owl and the Nightingale' was written. Andreas Capellanus, the queen's chaplain, had at her request composed his treatise, *De Arte Honeste Amandi*, which was to become a handbook for lovers and, naturally, was to incur condemnation by the Church, in spite of Andreas's renunciation of the ideas contained in it. In the first part of the poem, the Nightingale goes strictly 'by the book', even to the extent of approving the extra-marital lovings in the lays of Marie de France.[15]

This standard courtly-love philosophy the Owl opposes with a mixture of morbidity, realism and ridicule. She notes the connection between summer-time and lechery, and pushes home her distinction between lust and love with a huge joke at the expense of jaded lovers. I think the realism of her subsequent charge that the Nightingale perches by the privy (ll. 583-96) has been missed by critics generally; the nature of physical love, she is suggesting, contains something which all the Nightingale's lofty trillings tend to obscure – bodily function. Yeats's well-known lines illuminate the per-

15. D. W. Robertson Jr. (*A Preface to Chaucer: Studies in Medieval Perspectives*, Princeton U.P., 1962, pp. 391-503) suggests that Capellanus is using erroneous thought and practice in matters of love to recommend, often ironically, a loftier, Christian, doctrine. But C. S. Lewis, in *The Allegory of Love* (Oxford University Press, 1936), remarks that Capellanus' conclusion is palinodal (p.41) in finally recommending the opposite courses to those he has proposed throughout his thesis.

ception that 'fair and foul are near of kin' less pejoratively than the Owl:

> But Love has pitched his mansion in
> The place of excrement;
> For nothing can be sole or whole
> That has not been rent.[16]

The Owl's disposition to reject love and all its works during the bulk of the poem shows in her desire to console those afflicted by it, and to have those guilty of love intrigues cruelly punished (ll. 1045–67).

How different from these two set positions are the new ones adopted by the Nightingale and the Owl in their final confrontation! The Nightingale rejects adultery, and actually goes on to say:

> For virtuous wives in marriage grant
> Their husbands better loving than
> A wanton gives a fancy man.   (1340–42)

She presents the love her song incites in women and girls as pure essence, something as pure as the Owl's foreknowledge, which may be used either for good or for evil purposes. And if the purpose is evil, as when a woman's naturally soft heart makes her yield to a preying seducer, then the Nightingale dissociates herself from what she is now prepared to call 'an act of shame' (l. 1353). Love is 'the purest thing' (l. 1378) 'unless it's stolen' (l. 1380); yet one of the main attractions of courtly love was that it was secret, and hence, by implication, stolen. The Nightingale has surrendered the position she earlier defended with such spirit; which means, I believe, that her creator, impatient with the unreality of what was, after all, merely a literary convention,

16. W. B. Yeats: *Collected Poems* (Macmillan, 1950), p. 295.

wanted to speak his own views through her mouth, a thing he manages to do without outraging our sense either of what this particular nightingale is, or of the way she must conduct her side of the debate to her maximum advantage.

That is why we accept the Nightingale's moving plea on behalf of women who fall and then repent, and her passionate empathy with girls in love (ll. 1423–67). It might be said, with fair justice, that the only Christian quality missing from the Nightingale's final statement about love is a sacramental feeling for chastity; that phenomenon described by Helen Waddell as 'the grey cult of virginity'.[17]

The Owl, it might be thought, has no recantation to make as great as that of the Nightingale, because she is defending an orthodox position; but as we have seen, she has been accused of cruelty, of delighting in adversity and, lastly and much to her horror (ll. 1396–1416), of spiritual pride. Moreover, the poet, no doubt as impatient with the inflexibility of the formal position of the Owl as he was with that of the Nightingale, has also to speak his own views through the graver bird's mouth. The result is that the Owl, in a rare burst of compassion, admits justification for adultery when a husband is particularly worthless, and prays

> to Christ to grant them grace,
> To cure their woes and make them true,
> And send them better husbands too.   (1568–70)

Her compassion for, and empathy with, sorrowing wives at least matches the Nightingale's feeling for young girls bewildered by love. Significantly, in the tale which supplies the Owl with her example, 'A Penyworth of Wytt', the good wife did not cuckold her husband.

This virtual exchange of positions between the Owl and the Nightingale at the close of the debate, on a matter as

17. op. cit., p. 15.

important as adultery, surely indicates the poet's conviction that a decision on the outcome of the contest has become irrelevant; might indeed be harmful to a listener who has followed the arguments closely. For the Owl and the Nightingale have been brought to a point of synthesis. Their perorations, taken together, bind three main things: Latin recognition of the interaction of the spiritual and sensual in love; the ecstatic sense of being which is equally the attribute of courtly love and the medieval Church; and a common-sense, wise morality. These, brought together in a spirit of compassionate and realistic humanity, make a satisfactory synthesis independent of the strict formal positions of courtly love and the Church. Having regard to the expectations set up earlier, the poem thus ends, structurally speaking, with a deliberate anti-climax. It is of the essence of civilized comic writing, for it forces the reader to detach from the meretricious excitements and rigidities of partisanship, and to concentrate on the intellectual and moral issues raised, in an atmosphere made sane by laughter.

THE OWL AND THE NIGHTINGALE

It happened in the summery heart
Of a secret vale's most hidden part,
I heard an Owl and Nightingale
Disputing on a mighty scale;
Most keen and strenuous the debate,
Now gentle, now in furious spate.
And each against the other swelled,
Each her spleen and ire expelled,
Saying the worst of every feature
That she could mock in the other creature;
Contention was especially strong
When each abused the other's song.

      The first to speak, the Nightingale,
In a corner of the vale
Was perched upon a pretty twig
Where blossom showed on every sprig
And, fast entwined with reeds and sedge,
There grew a thick and lovely hedge.
She sang her varying tuneful lay,
Delighting in that flowering spray.
It seemed the melody she made
Was on a pipe or harpstring played,
That pipe or harp, not living throat,
Was shooting forth each pleasant note.
Nearby there stood a stump alone,
Decayed, with ivy overgrown,

And here the Owl had made her den,
And here sang out her 'hours' to men.[1]

  The Nightingale surveyed the Owl,
And reckoned her opponent foul;
Indeed all men declare with right
That she's a hideous, loathsome sight.
'Monster!' she cried, 'Away! Fly off!
Simply to see you's quite enough
To make me lose the urge to sing,
You're such an ugly, evil thing.
When you thrust out before my eyes,
My tongue is tied, my spirit dies,
Because your filthy clamouring
Makes me rather spit than sing.'

  The Owl held back till evening fell:
Then, as her heart began to swell,
Her breath to catch, her rage to grate,
She felt she could no longer wait,
And straight away exploded, 'How
Does this my singing strike you now?
D'you think I have no singing skill
Merely because I cannot trill?
You're always loading me with blame,
Girding at me with mock and shame.
If you were off that twig of yours,
And I could get you in my claws
(And would I could is all my boon),
You'd sing a different kind of tune.'

  To this the Nightingale replied,
'So long as I can safely hide

1. i.e. the canonical hours of prayer. These are defined in lines
323–8, when the Owl is defending her song by explaining its religious utility.

And shield myself against the cold
In quiet within this hedge's fold,
I neither attend to what you say,
Nor hear your threatenings with dismay.
I know how cruelly you attack
Small birds who cannot fight you back;
At every opportunity
You peck and tear them wantonly.
And that is why all birds detest you,
Why when they find you they molest you,[2]
Screeching and crying as they chase
And mob you till you leave the place.
Even the tiniest of the tits
Would gladly tear you into bits!
For you are loathsome through and through
And wholly hateful to the view:
Your neck is thin, your body squat,
Your head much bigger than the lot.
Your eyes are black as coal, and broad,
As if they had been daubed with woad.[3]
You glare as if you'd gorge on such
As come within your talons' clutch.
Your beak is hooked and sharp and strong,
A buckled awl, its shape gone wrong.
With it you gabble loud and long,
And that is what you call your song.

2. The mobbing of the Owl by smaller birds is described in
Book 10 of Pliny's *Natural History*, and was a common subject in
medieval art. Representations of it survive in churches, in both
stone and wood.

3. Woad is blue. The Nightingale's charge is one of barbarism,
because woad was used by primitive peoples, including early
Britons, for personal decoration.

Then, with your claws you threaten to slash
And pound my body to a mash.
The frog that sits by the mill-house wheel[4]
Would make a far more natural meal,
And snails and mice and such foul brood
Appear to be your proper food.
You perch by day and fly by night,
And that's not natural or right.
Most foul you are and most unclean:
Your nest shows clearly what I mean,
For there you rear your noisome brood
On dirty putrefying food;
And you know what they do with it:
They foul themselves chin-deep and sit
Amid the muck as if quite blind,
Which brings this pithy saying to mind:
"Ill fortune take that thing unblest,
The bird who fouls his own nest."
A falcon once, the eggs being laid,[5]
Neglected them, and was betrayed,
For there one day by stealth you flew
And laid your filthy egg there too.

4. Marie de France refers in one of her fables to a frog living
under a mill-wheel – a good place for a creature so often anthro-
pomorphized in beast-fable. C. Sisam (*Review of English Studies*,
November 1962, pp. 143–6) notes that owls do in fact swallow
frogs, and relates a miraculous cure performed by Ailred (d. 1167).
A young man had swallowed a very little frog while drinking
water, and this frog grew inside him daily, eating away his en-
trails. He grew enormously swollen, and *neckless like an owl*. Poor
chap, he must have been glad to be cured.

5. Another traditional fable found in Marie de France; but the

In course of time, the hatching done,
The nestlings came out one by one,
And soon the falcon brought them meat.
He guarded them and watched them eat,
And saw the outside of the nest
At one point had been foully messed.
Then sternly chiding was his mood:
He screamed in fury at his brood,
"Which of you have done this deed
Unnatural to our kind of breed?
Some foulness has been done to you:
Let him who knows it tell me true!"
At last one said, and then another,
"I think in truth it was our brother,
That fellow with the outsize head.
(If it were off, then he'd be dead!)
Let's throw him out with all our scraps,
So that his rotten neck-bone snaps!"
The falcon took them at their word
And seizing the repulsive bird,
Flung him from the treetop nest,
And crow and magpie did the rest.
From this men make a parable
Not lengthy, but of meaning full:
So fares the man of evil fame
Whose family bears no good name;
He may among the lordly go
But whence he came will always show –
That addle egg from which he fell,
Though in a noble nest he dwell.

-----

poet uses details from several different versions. The preceding
proverb is found in many languages.

The apple rolls from the parent tree
It shared with others of its degree;
But though it roll and trundle far,
It must show what its origins are.'[6]

  The Nightingale, her discourse spun,
And all her long indictment done,
Then sang in tones as loud and sharp
As if she'd plucked a plangent harp.
The Owl was listening to the sound,
Her big eyes fixed upon the ground,
And sat as swollen on her log
As if she'd gobbled up a frog.
The Nightingale's loud music she
Well knew was sung in mockery,
And yet the Owl at once replied,
'Then let us flying side by side
Go to the open field and see
Who is more lovely, you or me.'[7]

  'Your claws,' the night-bird said, 'are keen.
I'd rather not be caught between
Such mighty talons squeezing me
Like tongs in their rapacity.
You thought like others of your kind,
With well-bred words to lull my mind.

6. This proverb is associated with the Owl and Falcon fable in
Marie de France, but Aelfric, writing before the Norman Conquest, uses it. Marie de France claimed that her fable material
came from Alfred's collection.

7. The Owl is proposing trial by combat, 'which was introduced into England by the Normans and remained in force until
1219' (Atkins, *The Owl and the Nightingale*, Cambridge U.P.
1922, p. 15n.). The clergy regarded it with disfavour.

But your advice I'd never follow,
For well I know your faith is hollow.
Shame on you for your fake advice!
Now all can note your treacherous lies.
If evil's what you wish to do,
Take care to hide it from the view;
Shield your treachery from the light
And hide the wrong beneath the right.
For treachery brings but hate and gall
If it is plainly shown to all.
You cannot win with such a trick,
For I can dodge it, fleet and quick;
Nor will your courage bring success,
For I can fight with craftiness
Which has more use than all your strength.
I have besides in breadth and length
This splendid fort of hedge. The wise
Say, "He fights well who shrewdly flies."
But let us stop our little squabble,
For there's no point in all this babble.
Let us conduct a proper trial,
Using courteous speech the while,
For though we may not be agreed,
We may with due decorum plead,
And so, without a wordy fight,
Proceed with truth towards the right.
And each may say what she intends
With reason and for sanctioned ends.'
        'But,' said the Owl, 'who can secure
For us a judgement fair and sure?'
        'I know,' the Nightingale replied,
'The very man. Don't quibble or chide.

Master Nicholas is his name,
From Guildford, one of lofty fame[8]
For wisdom, prudence, judgement nice –
A foe to every kind of vice.
Then too, he has the music skill,
Knows who sings well and who sings ill.
He can distinguish wrong from right
And things of dark from things of light.'

    The Owl took time to think this out,
But thus at last resolved her doubt;
'I think that he will judge with truth,
For though he spent an ardent youth,
Delighting in the nightingale
And other creatures small and frail,
I know that now his spark is cooled.
No likelihood that he'll be fooled
And, prompted by his former love,
Put me beneath and you above.
There's nothing now that you can do
To stop his judgement being true.
His mind is settled and mature
And proof against the pleasure lure.
No more he seeks diversions gay,
For he pursues the righteous way.'

    The Nightingale was ready for this,
Being schooled in witty artifice.
'Owl,' she exclaimed, 'Now tell me true:
Why behave as monsters do,

8. For discussion of Nicholas of Guildford, see Appendix
p. 250-51. The title 'Master' was allowed, of courtesy, to all those
admitted to the higher faculties of the universities of Oxford and
Cambridge.

Singing by night and not by day?
You wail and yell the night away,
And certainly you terrify
Every soul that hears you cry.
You screech and hoot to all your kin,
Making a dreadful, grisly din;
And sage and fool agree, old Owl,
That you don't sing, but simply howl.
You fly by night and not by day.
I wonder why, and well I may,
For every thing that shuns the right
Loves the dark and hates the light,
And every thing inclined to sin
Prefers the dark for working in.
A maxim wise but unrefined
King Alfred spoke, and so we find
It often voiced: "A man will shun
Those who know he's a dirty one."
For you this is exactly right,
Because you always fly by night.
Another thing occurs to me:
Night's the time when you best see.
By day you're blind, or so you seem,
And can't distinguish tree or stream.
Your utter blindness in the day[9]
Is made a parable. Men say,
"The evil man is just like this,
For things of good he's sure to miss.

9. Owls can of course see by day, although, as T. H. White remarks (op. cit., p. 248): 'In public houses the English peasantry are at this moment assuring one another that owls cannot see in daylight.'

None can avoid the tricks he plays,
So foul and wicked are his ways.
Darkness is the road he knows,
And where light is, he never goes."
That is the way of all your kind:
They never have the light in mind.'

      The Owl had grown distinctly vexed
While listening, and protested next:
'I know that Nightingale's your name
But "Chatterbox"[10] would suit your fame
Because you have too much to say:
Tie down your tongue for a holiday!
You think all day belongs to you,
But I must have my own time, too,
So hold your peace and let me speak;
To take revenge is what I seek.
Observe how in my own defence
I speak with point and truth and sense.
You swear I hide myself by day,
And that I never shall gainsay.
So listen to me while I try
To tell the wherefore and the why.
I have a beak that's big and strong,
And splendid claws both sharp and long,
Which for the race of hawks is right.
It is my custom and delight
To lead the life to which I'm born;
At this no man can gibe in scorn.
In me it can be clearly seen
That Nature made me fierce and keen,

10. The original word is *galegale*, a ludicrous coining by the
author, based on the meaning of the last syllable of the word
'nightingale', which is 'sing'.

And loathed by little birds who fly
Low down and in the thickets ply.
They make a screaming, twittering sound
And flock in force to mob me round;
But I prefer to stay at rest,
Sitting quietly in my nest.
What profit should I then produce
By routing them with loud abuse,
Reviling them with shout and curse
As foul-mouthed shepherds do, or worse?
Upbraiding shrews affords few joys,
So I keep clear of all their noise.
There is a proverb wise in word;
On sages' lips it's often heard:
"To rail at fools brings only scorn,
Like trying to match an oven's yawn."
Another time I heard one quote
A maxim that King Alfred wrote:
"As for scolding, brawls and strife,
Avoid the place where they are rife.
Let fools contend, and go your way."
These words of wisdom I obey.
And Alfred said, still yet again,
A maxim widely known to men:
"He who meddles with what is mean
Never escapes entirely clean."
What harm do crows do to the hawk,
When in the marsh they cry and squawk,
Approaching him with rasping caw
As if they wished to start a war?
The hawk removes himself, being wise,
And leaves them with their grating cries.

'Besides, another lie you tell
Is that I cannot sing too well,
But have a doleful voice and drear,
The sound of which is harsh to hear.
You lie: my voice in very truth
Is blithe, melodious and smooth.
You think that every voice is foul
Which differs from your squeaky howl.
My voice is masterful and strong,
And like a mighty horn in song,
While yours is like a tiny pipe
Fashioned from a reed unripe.
My voice is greatest, yours is least;
You chatter like an Irish priest.[11]
I sing at eve, when song is due,.
Give utterance at bed-time too,
And then at midnight once again,
And lastly lift my glad refrain
When I see rising from afar
In light of dawn, the morning star.[12]
And so my song brings benefit,
Forewarning men with message fit,
But you sing all the livelong night
From evening time till morning light.
No matter that the night is long,
You always sing the selfsame song.
You never rest your wretched voice,
But fill the night and day with noise,

11. A number of pejorative references to Irish clergy in medi-eval English have been noted by G. G. Coulton.

12. The Owl here specifies the canonical hours at which she calls the clergy to prayer: Vespers ('at eve'), Compline ('at bed-time'), Matins ('at midnight'), and Lauds ('in light of dawn').

And constantly assault the ear,
So that people living near
Become so hostile to the din
They reckon it not worth a pin.
Thus pleasure can be overdone
And last so long it gladdens none.
For harp's, or pipe's, or bird's sweet song
Displeases if kept up too long;
However glad the song may be,
It brings delight in no degree
To him who hears against his will.
So I suggest your tongue be still.
For it is time, as Alfred said,
And in a book it may be read,
"The virtue of a thing grows less
By overdoing and excess."
Satiety corrupts all pleasure:
Disgust attends on lack of measure.[13]
There's no delight that I can name[14]
Which will survive if kept the same

13. A proverb of wide distribution, which finds formal expression in many philosophical and religious systems. The work of Aristotle is full of commonsense applications of the idea, which were given a Christian emphasis (sometimes amounting to a twist) by Aquinas. The proverb seems to be the key one in the whole poem: the degree to which each bird over-states her case tends to be the measure of the alienation of the reader's sympathy.

14. The Owl here takes on the role of a homilist, using the conventional style and material of a preacher. The comparison of the Kingdom of God with a basket reads like a parable of the Kingdom, for which one naturally searches the Bible. But it is an original one as far as can be ascertained; the only container in the Bible which automatically re-fills at divine behest is the widow's

Except the Kingdom of God above,
Unchanging in its endless love.
That basket, when you've seized your fill,
Is full to overflowing still;
God's kingdom, wonderful in fame,
Gives ceaselessly, yet stays the same.
                    'You mock me with another slur,
To my defective eyes refer,
Because, you say, I fly by night
And cannot see when it is light.
But there you lie, for it is clear
In seeing I can have no peer,
Because however dark the night,
I penetrate it with my sight.
You think because it is my way
To fly by night, I'm blind by day.
But then by day the hare lies low,
Whose vision is faultless, even so.
If he is hounded by the pack,
He winds his way by narrow track,
Escaping by a motion quick,
Exploiting every clever trick,

---

cruse (1 Kings xvii, 12–16). I am indebted to the Rev. Professor
M. F. Wiles for this comment: 'Tertullian (*Adversus Marcionem*
iv, 21) does link the feeding of the five thousand and the widow's
cruse in a typically allusive way in the course of arguing the similarity of God's actions in the Old and New Testaments, but there
is no reference to re-filling of baskets or anything of that sort.
Hilary (*De Trinitate* III, 16) gives an imaginative description of
the bread multiplying itself in the process of distribution in his
account of the feeding of the five thousand.'

Hopping and leaping from the chase
Until he finds his hiding place.
He could not so effect his flight
Unless his eyes possessed good sight.
And I can see, just like the hare,
And stay in daytime in my lair.
When valiant men prepare for war,
Then go campaigning near and far,
And overrun the folk they fight,
They often operate by night,
And then I follow such bold thanes,
Accompanying their battle trains.'[15]

    The Nightingale took this to heart
And wondered long how she could start
An answer to the case she'd heard,
For what the Owl had just averred
Was wise and sound, and would defy
The best rebuttal she could try.
Regretting then that she had spent
So long a time in argument,
She was afraid that her retort
Might very well fall somewhat short.
She spoke out still, quite unafraid,
For he is wise who, undismayed,
Confronts his foe with steadfast face,
Avoiding fear, with its disgrace.
The foe who yields to bravery
Will yet be bold if you should flee,
But if he sees your heart is big,
He'll change from boar to gelded pig;

15. Accompanying warriors is one of the functions of the hawk, with whom the Owl claims kinship. But the chief creatures of battle are the eagle, the raven and the wolf.

So, though she felt inclined to quail,
Thus boldly spoke the Nightingale:
    'Owl!' she said, 'Why do you so?
You sing your winter song of woe,
Clucking out your grief to men
Just like a wretched snow-bound hen.
In winter loud and cross you sing;
In summer you're dumb as anything.
You can't rejoice with all the rest,
Being by grudging hate possessed.
When joy and bliss spread wide and free
You're eaten up by jealousy.
You're like the man of evil spite
To whom all joy's a loathsome sight;
Who frowns and frets and grumbles when
By chance he sees contented men.
That fellow rather would behold
Tears in the eyes of young and old,
And wooltufts might, for all he'd care,
Be tangled topknots, threads and hair.[16]
That's just like you: when far and wide
The snow lies thick on every side,
And all mankind is sunk in sorrow,
You sing from evening till the morrow.
But I bring with me joy and glee,
For men are cheered because of me,
Rejoice the moment I appear,
Are glad before I'm even near.

16. A passage obscure in the original, though the general sense
is clear. The 'man of spite' is content merely to contemplate the
weaver faced by a tangled mass of different impurities when he is
trying to produce good wool.

The blossom springs upon the tree,[17]
And flowers spread on field and lea;
The lily with her lovely show
Welcomes me, as well you know,
And with her beauty bids me stir,
And calls to me to fly to her.
The rose as well, with tint of red,
From out the briar-bush shows her head,
And then she asks if I will sing,
For love of her, some pleasant thing.
And this I do, both night and day:
The more I sing, the more I may,
Delighting people with my song,
Though never going on too long.
For when I see that men are glad,
I do not wish them to be sad.
But having thus achieved my aim,
I wisely go back whence I came.
When man reflects on harvest sheaves
And autumn colours stain the leaves,
I say farewell and homeward flee,
For winter's ruin is not for me.
When bitter weather is at hand,
Home I go to my own land,

17. The Nightingale substantiates her claim to be representative
of happiness and spring by presenting her argument at this point
in the language of the spring love-lyric. In Anglo-Saxon and
early medieval times, the cuckoo was of course the bird of spring.
The nightingale challenged the cuckoo's position when the
French influence brought in the teaching of Pliny on this point.
But the cuckoo seems to have won in the end, to judge by her
domination of Elizabethan spring poetry and song.

Taking love and thanks, my gains
For having come and taken pains.
Should I remain, my task being done?
No fear! For reason there is none.
For he has neither sense nor wit
Who stays when there's no need of it.'

     The listening Owl took every word,
Storing up the speech she'd heard,
And then considered how she might
Discover means to answer right,
For he who fears a lawyer's guile
Must ponder in himself awhile.

     'You ask me,' was the Owl's reply,
'Why in winter I sing and cry.
It is the usual thing for man,
And has been since the world began,
To recognize and cheer his friends,
Rejoicing in their common ends,
With cordial talk and kindly word
Within his house and at his board.
At Christmas is this specially so,
When rich and poor, and high and low,
Sing their dance-songs night and day,[18]
And I take part in every way.
I think as well of many a thing
Besides the need to play and sing.
And this is how I answer you,
Prompt and ready on my cue:

---

18. The kind of Christmas song named, the *cundut* (Latin: *conductus*), was a song for tenor and two other voices, originally sung while the priest moved towards the altar, but converted to secular use.

The summer time's too full of pride:[19]
It turns a good man's thoughts aside
From wholesomeness and purity
To concentrate on Lechery.
Wild animals will not stay still,
But ramp and mount and mate at will.
The fiery stallions in the stud
Rage for mares with all their blood.
And you with all these wantons throng,
For lust's the subject of your song.
When you're just about to mate,
You're full of fire and passionate.
But when you've done your treading act
You cannot speak, and that's a fact.[20]
Your voice has got a crack in it –
You twitter hoarsely, like a tit.
You sing worse then than sparrows do
Who fly low down and flutter through
The scrub and stumps. So one can tell
Your lust is gone, your song as well.

19. E. G. Stanley thinks summer is personified here, as winter may be in line 458. See Introduction, p. 159.

20. More unnatural history. Albertus Magnus (d. 1280), says E. G. Stanley, wrongly attributed the statement to Pliny, but the idea is widely mentioned, and is in harmony with the mythology of sex generally. St John Gogarty's poem 'After Galen' comments amusingly:

> 'Only the Lion and the Cock,
> As Galen says, withstand Love's shock.
> So, Dearest, do not think me rude
> If I yield now to lassitude,
> But sympathize with me. I know
> You would not have me roar, or crow.'

In fact, the Nightingale sings until the young are hatched.

In summer peasants lose their sense
And jerk in mad concupiscence:
Theirs is not love's enthusiasm,
But some ignoble, churlish spasm,
Which having achieved its chosen aim,
Leaves their spirits gorged and tame.
The poke beneath the skirt is ended,
And with the act, all love's expended.
Just so, it seems your singing mood
Goes flabby when you sit and brood:
You lose all sense of melody
And when you're perched upon a tree,
Your joy being sung, it's just the same:
The discords only bring you shame.
But in the winter of the year
When long dark nights bring frost severe,
Distinctly people may observe
Who keeps his vigour and his verve!
And times reveal to us what kind
Thrusts boldly on, what lags behind:
Adversity throws up the one
By whom the task of worth is done.
And then's the time I sing with zest,
And play in pleasure manifest.
Winter worries me not at all,
For I'm no abject, drooping thrall,
But one who brings relief to those
Who lack the strength to bear their woes,
Who sit and think in misery
And long for warmth most eagerly.
For them I sing, and sing again
To bring some easement of their pain.

Have I caught you now, poor bird?
Trapped you with a truthful word?'
     'Indeed not,' said the Nightingale:
'You shall hear another tale.
No judgement yet for our debate!
So listen while I put you straight.
One word from me will stultify
The logic that you seek to apply.'
     'Illegal!' cried the Owl. 'You prayed
To sue me, then the charge you laid,
And to the charge I have replied.
Before the judgement is applied,
I am resolved that I'll charge you
As you charged me, or meant to do.
So answer, if you're able to.
Tell me now, you rascal, you,
Do you possess a thing of note
Besides your ever-shrilling throat?
You have no use or skill at all
Except your power to caterwaul.
Yes, you're undersized and frail;
Your weak defence is sure to fail.
And as for doing good to men,
You hardly match the feeble wren.
Nothing positive, it seems,
You offer but demented screams.
And then when all your squeaking's done,
Other resources have you none.
Alfred the wise expressed this view
(And well he might, for it is true)
"No one is honoured very long
Merely because he sings a song:

Indeed, that man's not worth a thing
Whose only talent is to sing."
"Not worth a thing" applies to you,
Since chatter is all you ever do.
Besides, you're filthy, dark and small,
Like a sort of sooty ball.[21]
You have no loveliness or strength,
And lack harmonious breadth and length.
Beauty somehow passed you by;
Your virtue, too, 's in short supply.
And let me tell you something more:
Your looks and habits are impure.
Perceiving man's enclosure place,
Where thorns and branches interlace
To form a thickly hedged retreat
For man to hide his privy seat,
There you go, and there you stay;
From clean resorts you keep away.
When nightly I pursue the mouse,
I catch you by the privy house
With weeds and nettles overgrown –
Perched at song behind the throne.
Indeed you're likely to appear
Wherever humans do a rear.
And yet you blame me for my meat:
Foul beasts, you say, are what I eat.
But what's your own diet (tell no lies!)
But spiders and revolting flies?
And bugs you also chance to seize
From crevices in the bark of trees.

21. The nightingale's undistinguished colouring does in fact
contrast with its distinctive song.

But my purveyance is designed
To help the hearth of humankind.
I give them aid: and that is good,
Because I help them with their food.
Nightly in God's holy house
And in the barns, I hunt the mouse.
I love to cleanse of filthy mice
The church beloved beyond all price.
If I can stop it, I declare
That nothing vile shall enter there.
But since I please to take delight
In dwelling far from human sight,
I pick a mighty tree for lair
With sturdy branches never bare,
So green with ivy intertwined
That year-long blossom comes to mind;
Its lovely hue is never lost
When winter comes, through snow or frost.
A splendid fastness there I rule,
In winter, warm; in summer, cool.
So when my den is bright and green,
In yours there is no colour seen.
You also raise another matter,
Attack my young with mocking chatter,
Complaining that their nest's unclean.
But this in other beasts is seen,
For horse in stable, ox in stall,
Excrete at will, as do we all.
A tiny baby in a cot,
Whether noble or base his lot,
Performs as best a baby can,
But disciplines it when a man.

How can a baby hold it in?
The unavoidable's no sin.
This ancient proverb you should heed:
"Even a hag will trot at need."
Yet one thing more. May I request
That you proceed to see my nest?
If you're wise, you'll understand
The principles on which it's planned.
The middle, my babies' dwelling place,
Is soft and cosy, full of space.
But on the outside of the nest
All is plaited firm and pressed,
And that is where their stool is rid,
Not where you say, which I forbid.
We note the style of human bowers
And similarly fashion ours.
Men, *inter alia*, have designed
An outhouse privy which they find
Without a tedious walk. Just so
My owlets find it good to go.
Now sit still, squawker, and don't fret;
You've never been so hard beset.
You won't be able to reply.
Hang up your axe, and say good-bye.'

      The Nightingale, at this effusion,
Was almost speechless with confusion,
And furiously gave her mind
To think what talent she could find
Apart from singing, to produce
Some other benefit or use.
An answer she must surely find
Or utterly be left behind.

And certainly it's hard to fight
Against the truth, against the right.
When the heart is cornered, man
Must use whatever guile he can.
In speech he must dissimulate
And cough and hem, procrastinate,
In order that the mouth conceal
What heart might otherwise reveal.
A word may tear a case apart
When mouth speaks out against the heart,
And, heart being out of key with tongue,
A speech can suddenly go wrong.
Yet all the same, for him who knows,
Even here some comfort shows.
For human wit is never so keen
As when the problem's unforeseen.
It's when the mind is most in fear
That guile and cunning first appear.
For Alfred long ago averred
(And men have not forgotten his word):
'When tribulations menace men,
Their remedies are nearest then.'
For wit and understanding grow
In time of woe, because of woe.
So man should never lack advice
As long as sense and wit suffice:
But when his sense is derelict
His wisdom-pocket will be picked;
No hope of any counsel-pence
If he cannot keep his sense.
This, Alfred said, because he knew
And always uttered what was true:

'When tribulations threaten men,
Their remedies are nearest then.'
Just so the Nightingale had sought
To give the case her utmost thought.
Now, under stress and under strain,
Her ponderings brought good sense again,
Until the wit with which she fought
Produced at last the right retort.

      'Owl,' she said, 'You asked me what
Accomplishment or skill I've got
But singing in the summer-tide
And giving pleasure far and wide.
Why ask, when all your skills are less
Than that one art that I possess?
One song from me's worth more than all
The songs the whole of owl-kind bawl.
The reason, if you'll hear, is this:
Mankind was born for heavenly bliss,
(Did you know that of human birth?)
And heaven has endless song and mirth.
Thus every man of virtuous skill
Hurries there with all his will.
And thus in holy church men sing,
And priests compose their offering,
That song may keep in each man's mind
The eternal home that he shall find;
That he may not forget that bliss,
But think of it and make it his.
And thus they heed the Church's lore
That heaven is joy for evermore.
In every cloister round about
Priests, monks and canons, all devout,

Will leave their beds at dead of night
To sing the bliss of heaven's light,
And lay-priests[22] too take up the song
When beams of dawn begin to throng.
I help them all as best I may[23]
By singing with them night and day.
They're happier because of me
And chant and sing more readily.
I predispose them to their good
By helping on their joyous mood,
And pray that each one may attain
The joy of heaven's eternal strain.
So sit and shrivel up, you Owl!
No subject this for you to howl!
The case between us must be tried,
So let the Pope in Rome[24] decide.
But let us not go quite so fast;
You shall endure another blast
Of words that you will not resist
For all of England, I insist.
You twit me for my lack of strength,
My lack of size and lack of length,
And then declare I am not strong
Because I'm neither big nor long.

22. Lay priests were allowed to conduct services only by day.

23. The tradition that the nightingale sings in praise of God seems to have begun in Charlemagne's time.

24. Some have argued that the legal battle of the poem is conducted according to secular rules, but E. G. Stanley convincingly uses this reference to the Pope, and other evidence, to show that ecclesiastical law is followed. The 'impetration of a papal writ is a regular first step in English canon law,' he writes (*The Owl and the Nightingale*, Nelson, 1960, p. 29).

Your meaning there is most obscure:
You utter only lies, I'm sure.
Cunning I have, and also art,
And therefore am I bold of heart;
Both wit and song-craft I possess;
To them alone I owe success.
And this is Alfred's truth: that might,
When matched with skill, must lose the fight.
A little skill will often prevail
When mighty strength's of no avail.
Often the tower or city wall
By guile, not strength, is made to fall.
By guile the bravest knights are thrown
And towering ramparts toppled down.
Brute force turns worthless in a trice,
But wisdom always holds its price.
Wherever you direct your eyes,
You'll find no equal to the wise.
A horse is stronger than a man,
But lacking wit, it only can
Bear burdens on its back and lead
Great teams of horses, which proceed
Under the scourge of stick and spur.
Or tied up by the mill-house door,
It does whatever men command,
And since it cannot understand,
It must despite its strength obey
What even tiny children say.
But man contrives by strength and sense
That nothing has his eminence.
And though all brute strengths join their skill,
The guile of man is greater still,

For human wit and penetration
Master all the brute creation.
One song from me outclasses all
Your dreary year-long caterwaul;
Men love me for my singing art,
But hate you for your violent heart.
So why d'you think the worse of me
For having one sole faculty?
If two wrestlers start a fight
And both men try with all their might,
But one has many kinds of throw
Which only he can use and know,
And the other has a single plan
By which he always beats his man,
Giving his enemy the fall
In hardly any time at all,
Why should he learn another skill
When this one makes him win at will?
You say that I am unlike you
With all the useful things you do.
But take your tricks and pile them all;
Beside my single skill they're small.
When hounds hunt foxes in a pack,
The cat is safe from all attack,
Although he has but one resort.
The fox has tricks of every sort,
But none so good as to confound
Every single pursuing hound.
He knows the straight and devious way,
And how to send the hounds astray
By hanging from a bough,[25] that so,

25. Since this climbing of trees is the very trick the singularity
and effectiveness of which distinguish the cat, the Nightingale,

The scent being lost, away they go.
The fox can quickly double back,
Or creep by hedges, change his track,
And set the hound upon a trail
Where the scent is sure to fail.
Forward and back, the scents confound
The wits of the pursuing hound.
If all these dodges miss their goal,
At last the fox can slink to hole.
Yet notwithstanding every wile,
Despite his swiftness, craft and guile,
Whatever his plans, when all is said,
He'll lose at last his fur of red.
The cat exploits a single skill
To save himself on fen or hill;
An excellent climber, he can stay
Aloft and save his fur of grey.
And so of my one skill I say,
It beats your twelve tricks any day.'

     'Hold hard! hold hard!' exclaimed the Owl,
'Your style in all is fake and foul.
You colour every single word
To sound like truth, you lying bird!
You round and polish all you say
In such an unctuous, specious way
That all who turn an ear to you
Suppose your utterance to be true.
Hold hard! you shall be countered yet!
Your mighty falsehoods shall be met

---

with either a knowing or an unconscious poet behind her, is defeating her own argument. Alexander Neckam mentions this
propensity of foxes, which is an actual, not imaginary one.

When they're exposed and clearly seen,
And all know what a liar you've been.
You say you sing to all mankind
Of blisses they should strive to find,
And of the everlasting choir –
How strange that such a bare-faced liar
As you should bluff so openly!
D'you think they'll come so easily
To God's high kingdom? By a song?
No, no. They'll surely find that long
And contrite weeping and a plea
For pardon for their sins will be
The only way to enter in.
I therefore say men should begin
To weep[26] much rather than to sing
If they yearn for heaven's king.
There's not a single man alive
Who's free of sin; so all should strive
With tears and weeping to atone
Till all sweet things to sour are grown.
I help this process on, God knows:
My songs no idiot[27] course propose,

26. It was standard religious teaching, emphasized by the Church Fathers and echoed by the schoolmen, that religious duty enjoined weeping. A seminal text is Psalms cxxvi. 6. The Owl, like a good monk, claims to make man weep for his sins, the sins of others, the sorrows of the world, and his longing for heaven.

27. The ME *foliot* ('foolish matter' according to Stratmann's *Middle English Dictionary*, but a device for catching birds such as a *trompe-oiseau* mirror or dummy bird according to E. G. Stanley) is a nonce-word. Since an enemy of Thomas à Becket was called Foliot (Bishop of London 1163–87), the fact has been used to make an interpretative key to fit the whole poem. Thus, in Anne Baldwin's interpretation (see Introduction, pp. 160–61) Foliot is Judas.

But teach the listening man to yearn
And make lament his chief concern.
For thus he heeds his mortal state
And groans because his sins are great.
I goad him on, by what I sing,
To wail his guilty trespassing.
If you dispute this, I reply
You sing less well than I can cry.
If right takes precedence over wrong,
My tears are better than your song.
Some men there are, both good and true
And pure in spirit through and through,
Who notwithstanding yearn to go
Because they find this life all woe.
Though saved themselves, on earth they see
Nothing but pain and misery.
They shed harsh tears for others' woes
And pray Christ's mercy come to those.
And thus I help both good and bad;
From me a two-fold grace is had.
My song helps virtuous men to yearn;
I sing when they with longing burn.
I help the bad no less, for I
In song instruct where sufferings lie.
With further blame your plea I twit:
For when upon your twig you sit,
You lure to fleshly lust and wrong
All those who listen to your song.
The bliss of heaven you quite ignore;
You have no voice for such a lore.
All your song's of wantonness;
In you is found no holiness.

Your squeaks no man alive would grant
To be a mass-priest's holy chant!
But still another charge I lay,
Which you must try and talk away.
Why don't you sing in foreign parts?[28]
That's where they need the lively arts.
You never sing in Irish lands
Nor ever visit Scottish lands.
Why can't the Norsemen hear your lay,
Or even men of Galloway?[29]
Of singing skill those men have none
For any song beneath the sun.
Why don't you sing to priests up there
And teach them how to trill the air,
And show them by your chirruping
How the heavenly angels sing?
Just like a useless spring you seem
That jets out by a flowing stream,
But leaves the neighbouring lowland dry,
And gushes off downhill to die.
But north and south I make my stand
And am well known in every land.
Yes, east and west, and far and near
I sing my duty loud and clear,
Advising men with instant clamour
To shun your song's alluring glamour.
My song most clearly tells mankind
To leave the life of sin behind;

28. The narrow extent of the nightingale's penetration north of the Channel was commented on by medieval writers, and has been confirmed by modern ornithologists.

29. For background to the northern countries mentioned here and in the passage beginning at line 995, see Introduction, pp. 169-170.

I bid them cease from self-deceit,
For it is better and more sweet
On earth to weep with woe and care
Than be the Devil's friend elsewhere.'

    By now the Nightingale was cross,
Ashamed and rather at a loss,
Because the Owl in her harangue
Had mocked the place in which she sang –
Behind the house among the weed
Where men relieve their bodies' need.[30]
But yet she sat and thought it through,
For in her heart of hearts she knew
That rage destroys wise counselling,
As Alfred says, that learned king:
'The hated man can't intercede;
The angry man's not fit to plead.'
For wrath stirs up the spirit's blood
With raging surges like a flood,
And overpowers the beating mind
Until with passion it is blind.
The spirit thus loses all its light,
Perceiving neither truth nor right.
All this, the bird well understood,
And waited for a calmer mood.
She'd speak much better, feeling quiet,
Than wrangling in a mood of riot.

    'Now listen to me, Owl,' said she,
'You'll trip: your path is slippery.
I flee behind the house, you say?
Of course, it's ours. What better way?

---

30. A belated reply to the Owl's charge in lines 592–6 now
follows.

Where lord and lady lie in love,
I sit and sing, close by, above.
Do you suppose wise men forsake
The high road for the muddy brake?
Or that the sun will shine no more
Because your nest has a filthy floor?
So why should I my true place quit
For a board with hole cut out of it,
And sing no longer near the bed
Where lord and lady lay the head?
It is my duty and my law
To follow the highest evermore.
And if you vaunt aloud your song,
And boast of yelling fierce and strong,
And say that's how you tell mankind
To weep and leave their sins behind,
My answer is, if all lamented,
Screaming out as if tormented,
And screeching like an Owl, at least
They'd terrify the parish priest.[31]
Man should be calm and not cry out,
Though tears for error are devout.
But when he honours Christ in song,
Man's praises should be loud and long:
Too loud and long can never be
For psalm and hymn sung fittingly.
You scream and wail; I sing with measure.
Your voice is tearful; mine gives pleasure.
Ever may you waste your breath
And squall as if you longed for death!

31. The Nightingale is ridiculing the Owl's claim (ll. 733-5)
to help the secular priesthood.

And may you howl your song accursed
Till both your eyes pop out and burst!
Of two, which is the better way,
That humans should be glum, or gay?
May you and I be ever so fated,
That you be glum, and I elated!
You ask me why I do not travel
To sing to strangers. What a cavil!
What should I do with folk to whom
Content and pleasure never come?
The land is poor, a barren place,
A wilderness devoid of grace,
Where crags and rocks pierce heaven's air,
And snow and hail are everywhere –
A grisly and uncanny part
Where men are wild and grim of heart.
Security and peace are rare,
And how they live they do not care.
The flesh and fish they eat are raw;
Like wolves, they tear it with the paw.
They take both milk and whey for drink;
Of other things they cannot think,
Possessing neither wine nor beer.
They live like wild beasts all the year
And wander clad in shaggy fell
As if they'd just come out of hell.
If some good man to them would come
– As once one came from holy Rome[32]

32. This has all the signs of a topical reference. Presumably it is
to the journey of Cardinal Vivian, who journeyed on a papal mis-
sion to Scotland, Ireland and Norway in 1176. But K. Huganir
(*The Owl and the Nightingale: Sources, Date, Author* 1931, pp. 108

To teach them virtue's better way
And help them shake off evil's sway –
He'd wish he'd stayed at home, I swear:
He'd only waste his time up there;
For he could get a bear[33] to wield
A spear and hold a warrior's shield
More easily than men so wild
To hear my song and be beguiled.
What use would be my singing there?
However long-drawn-out or fair,
It would be wasted, wholly idle.
Since not the halter, not the bridle,
Nor tool of iron or weapon of steel
Could bring such maddened dogs to heel.
But in a land of pleasant charm
Where folk are gentle, kind and calm,
I exercise my tuneful throat
And render services of note.
Glad tidings to such folk I bring;
The Church's hymns are what I sing.
It stated in the law of old
– That wisdom yet assures the fold –
The harvest that a man should mow
Is where he went to plough and sow,
For he is mad who sows his seed
Where grass and blossom cannot speed.'

     These words filled Owl with conflict dire;
Her eyes grew huge and rolled with ire.

---

ff.) suggests that the visit to Norway in 1152–4 of Nicholas
Breakspear, the only Englishman ever to become Pope, is meant.
  33. The bear was widely regarded as the type of cruelty.

'You say you guard man's homely bower
Adorned with leaf and fairest flower,
Where lovers lie in close embrace,
One bed their sheltered hiding place.
Once you sang – and I know where –[34]
Outside a certain house, and there,
By singing high and singing low
You taught the lady how to know
And do the lustful deed of shame –
Foul passion to her body's blame.
The lord, observing how things were,
Set bird-lime, traps and many a snare
To catch you at your little game,
And when to the lattice then you came,
A trap soon gripped you by the shins
And paid you out for all your sins.
Your doom was to be torn in bits
By raging horses: and it fits.
So if you try to soil the life
Again of virgin or of wife,
Expect your song to bring despair
And hopeless fluttering in a snare.'

34. The Owl and the Nightingale now comment in turn on a
well-known tale of courtly love which existed in many versions,
including one by Marie de France ('The Lay of the Austic'). The
essential details are that a lady in love with her knightly neighbour,
when suspected by her husband of leaving her room at night,
said that she went to hear the nightingale. The jealous lord had the
bird snared and, when the lady sorrowed, killed. In one version,
referred to by the poet's contemporary Alexander of Neckam, the
nightingale was drawn apart by four horses. Another similar tale
by Marie de France ('The Lay of Yonec') has the knightly lover
visit the lady in the shape of a falcon, which dies on spikes fixed to
the window by the jealous lord.

The Nightingale, enraged to hear
These words, with sword and point of spear
As human warrior would have fought,
But being unable, next she sought
The weapon of her prudent tongue.
'Who talks well fights well' once was sung.
And to her tongue she turned instead:
('Who talks well fights well' Alfred said.)
'You say all this to give me shame.
The husband got the final blame.
He was so jealous of his wife
He could not bear, to save his life,
To see her with a man converse,
For that would break his heart, or worse.
He therefore locked her in a room
– A harsh and savage kind of doom.
And this aroused my pity so
That I was sorry for her woe,
And often pleasured her with song,
Singing early, singing long.
And this enraged the jealous knight;
He hated me with purest spite.
He tried to put on me the blame,
But it redounded to his shame.
King Henry came to know of this –
May Christ preserve his soul in bliss![35]
And outlawed that suspicious knight,
Who out of evil wrath and spite
In such a worthy king's domain
Had made his wicked purpose plain

35. This blessing, which must refer to a dead King Henry, is important for the dating of the poem. See Appendix, p. 250.

By seizing one so small and thin
And robbing her of life and limb.
So honour came to all our kind.
The knight lost all, and he was fined
A hundred pounds,[36] which came to me.
Since then in blithe security
My birds have lived, as well they might,
In utmost joy and high delight.
With such revenge so well consoled,
Since then my speech has been more bold.
The precedent of that one case
Gives me my ever-happy face,
For I can lift my voice at will,
And none can do me any ill.
But you, you starveling! Stinking spook!
You cannot find a single nook
Or hollow log to cower in
Secure from foes who'll pinch your skin,
For boy and girl, master and groom,[37]
Conspire to bring about your doom.
When you sit still, they pouch up stones
And clods to pelt your ugly bones,
And then let fly until you're battered
Off your perch, your body shattered.

36. One hundred pounds would be four times the maximum
fine for homicide under the law. But Stanley suggests that the poet
simply means a huge sum of money.

37. If Stanley is right, the first pair of persons should be anti-
thetical as well as the second. He wonders whether 'boys of the
cloister and farmhands', rather than 'girls and boys' is the right
translation for *children*, *gromes*. Traditional enmities and dis-
tinctions are forgotten in common hate of the Owl.

And if you're toppled off or shot,
The first good use can then be got
From you, for, hoist upon a rod,
Your bag-shaped body, foul and odd,
Your ghastly neck, most surely scare
From cornfields birds who wander there.
You're useless, full of life and blood,
But as a scarecrow, pretty good.
For sparrow, goldfinch, rook and crow
Will never venture where they know
The seed's new-sown if on that land
Your carcase dangles close at hand.
When trees put forth their blooms in spring,
And young seeds come to burgeoning,
No bird will dare to pluck them if
You're hanging overhead all stiff.
Alive, you fill mankind with dread;
It's just the same when you are dead.
So surely now you realize
How your appearance terrifies
When you're alive and drawing breath,
Since dangling upside down in death
You still inspire the utmost awe
In those who screamed at you before.
And men are right to loathe you, for
You sing of troubles evermore.[38]
All that you sing of, soon or late,
Is men's misfortunes, which they hate.
When they have heard you screech at night
Most men are filled with dread and fright.

38. For a discussion of the part of the debate concerning astrology, see Introduction, pp. 171-3.

You sing when death is due to strike,
Or any woe that men dislike.
The loss of goods your song portends,
Or ruin and disgrace of friends.
Forays of warriors you foretell,
Thief-hunts and houses burnt as well.
Of farmers' coming woes you cry,
And hoot when stock is going to die.
Of husband's death you warn the wife,
And also herald legal strife.
You sing of man's disasters, so
Through you he comes to ruin and woe.
You never sing except when some
Adversity is bound to come,
And that is why men always shun you,
Why they pelt and beat and stun you
With sticks and stones and turf and clods –
Then your escape's against all odds.
Cursed be the beadle with his shout
Who spreads such wretched truths about!
Who always brings unpleasant news,
And burdens men with loathsome views!
May all who wear good linen cloth,[39]
And God as well, split you with wrath!'
    The Owl by no means waited long,
But quickly answered, stern and strong:
'What! Excommunicating me,
And not ordained? Or can you be?

39. Linen was not worn by the poor, nor by monks. The
Nightingale is therefore assuming she has support in cursing the
Owl, from prosperous people generally, including the higher
clergy. The Owl's quick rejoinder is based on the fact that only a
priest had the right to invoke God in laying a curse.

For sure, you do a priestly task.
Are you a priest? Or should I ask?
I don't know if you sing the mass;
Perhaps your holy curse might pass.
But surely it's your enmity
That puts this two-fold curse on me?
And so I easily reply,
"Go to!" Such was the carter's cry.[40]
Why twit me for my second sight,
My understanding and my might?
I have much wisdom and it's true
That I can read the future too.
Invasion, famine I foresee,
And what man's length of life shall be,
And when his death shall grieve his wife.
When feud and malice shall be rife,
And who's for hanging I can tell,
And other evil deaths as well.
When battle's joined and at the height,
I know which side will lose the fight.
Which cattle pestilence will kill,
And which wild beasts will soon lie still,
And whether bloom on trees will grow
Or corn will thrive; all these I know.
When houses shall be struck with fire,
Who'll fail, or gain his whole desire,
When ships will founder out at sea,

40. The cry in the text (*Drah to pe!*) has not been explained. It
could be a standard carter's command to his horse. But if so, its
relevance here is not clear. I have translated it as if it were something a carter might say to traffic coming in the opposite direction,
if he wanted to assert his right of way.

When smiths[41] will forge defectively:
These I predict, and much much more
I learn from studying written lore,
And I know more of Holy Writ
Than I will tell concerning it.
I often go to church and find
Much wisdom there to store my mind;
Symbolic meanings and much more
I understand from Bible lore.
And when they raise the hue and cry,[42]
I know before it starts, and why.
Hence, being so wise and full of wit,
Perturbed and sad I often sit
When trouble's looming over men,
And cry my loudest warning then.
I tell them that they must beware
And go about with utmost care.
On this, hear Alfred's weighty word
Which man should treasure once it's heard:
"Foresee your trouble in its course:
You thereby take away its force."
And violent blows strike much less hard
If he who takes them stays on guard.
An arrow watched right from the string
Will miss its mark, for if it wing
Directly at you, you can shy
And dodge and let it pass you by.

41. If (see discussion in Introduction, p. 172) the Owl is indeed listing calamities which happen under Saturn and Mars, there is special relevance in smiths, whose God is of course Mars, making faulty weapons and armour.

42. When the hue-and-cry was raised for a murderer or thief, all who heard it had to join the pursuit.

And if a man should come to shame,
What cause have I to take the blame?
For though I warn he'll be brought low,
It's not my fault that he is so.
Now, if you saw a blind man, pray,
Who could not find the proper way,
But swerved and fell into a ditch
All foul with mud and black as pitch,
D'you think he had a quicker fall
Because the Owl foresaw it all?
That's how foreknowledge works, I vow;
For when I sit upon my bough
I clearly see that dreadful woe
Is coming to some man below.
Should he who cannot see it approach
Load me, who can, with vile reproach?
For his hard fate should he blame me
Because I have more brain than he?
I'm right to shout when woes appear,
To warn mankind that they are near,
And plead with them to be on guard
Against misfortune cruel and hard.
But whether my noise be great or small
The will of God determines all.
So why am I complained of when
I tell of truths which trouble men?
And if I warned a year ahead
It wouldn't hasten them a shred.
I sing because I want all men
To know and understand that when
My hoots are heard I mean to say
Misfortune is not far away.

For no one can be wholly sure
That from all fears he is secure
And safe from all calamity:
And when it comes he cannot see.
For Alfred said, and wisely too,
For every word he spoke was true:
"The more a man's good fortunes grow,[43]
The greater caution he should show."
And then again: "Let no man trust
Too much to wealth that's on him thrust.
There's none so hot but comes to cold,
So white but turns to soiled and old,
So dearly loved but comes to hate,
So genial but turns irate.
Yes, everything that's transitory
Shall pass, like this world's ecstasy."
Now most clearly you can see
That you have spoken foolishly,
For things you say to give me shame
Rebound on you with all the blame.
Whatever happens, in every round
Your own throw fells you to the ground.
Your every word designed to offend
Adds to my honour in the end.
Try harder when you next begin,
Or more disgrace is what you'll win.'

43. This last recourse to proverbial lore (ll. 1271–80) shows the poet joining a number of proverbs into a connected philosophic statement. The two proverbs in lines 1271–5 are found in early English: the next four lines bear a general resemblance to a passage in *The Proverbs of Alfred*, and the final couplet sums up with a pessimism which may have been taken from standard medieval reading of Boethius's *De Consolatione Philosophiae*.

The Nightingale, in thoughtful plight,
Sat still and sighed, as well she might,
Considering what the Owl had said,
And to what end her pleading led.
Unsure and somewhat anxious, she
Worked out what her reply would be.
At last it came: 'What! Owl!' she said,
'Have you gone clean off your head?
Second sight is what you claim,
But you are ignorant whence it came.
If witchcraft was your magic guide,
Of that you must be purified
If with mankind you wish to stay:
If not, then you must fly away.
For all who had that evil skill[44]
Were cursed of old, and are cursed still,
As you are by the mouth of priest,
For from that crime you've never ceased.
I told you this not long ago;
Then fleeringly you asked to know
What ordination I'd gone through.
Such widespread curses fall on you
That if there were no priests about
You'd still be utterly cast out.
For certainly you are reviled,
Foul bird, by every man and child.

44. The Nightingale, desperately seeking a weakness in the Owl's argument, lays a charge of witchcraft, Christian hostility to which derives ultimately from 'Thou shalt not suffer a witch to live' (Exodus xxii, 18). There were many excommunications for witchcraft in England at about this time. Execution was a later development.

Now I have heard, and it is true,
Whoever can the future view
As you affirm you can, must be
A master of astrology.
But what do you know of any star,
You wretch, except that it is far?
But so do men and beasts, I'm sure;
Of such affairs they know no more.
An ape can open and shut a book,
Or turn its leaves, and on them look,
But yet he can't make head or tail
Of written words. You also fail
Because the stars you see so bright
Afford your gloomy mind no light.
And yet, vile thing, most viciously
You chide me and you censure me
For making song behind the house
And teaching wives to break their vows.[45]
Foul thing! Those words were falsely spoken;
Through me was wedlock never broken.
Yet true it is, where ladies throng,
And lovely girls, I sing my song.
And true it is of love I chant,
For virtuous wives in marriage grant
Their husbands better loving than
A wanton gives a fancy man.
A girl may take what man she chooses
And doing so, no honour loses,
Because she did true love confer
On him who lies on top of her.

45. For a discussion of courtly love and sexual morality in the
poem, see Introduction, pp. 174–80.

Such love as this I recommend:
To it, my songs and teaching tend.
But if a wife be weak of will –
And women are soft-hearted still –
And through some jester's crafty lies,
Some chap who begs and sadly sighs,
She once perform an act of shame,
Shall I for that be held to blame?[46]
If women will be so unchaste,
Why should the slur on me be placed?
I cannot cease to sing my airs
Because bad wives have love affairs.
A woman may frisk beneath the sheet
At will, with or without deceit,
And stirred to passion by my song,
She may do good, she may do wrong.
There's nothing good the whole world round
For which bad purpose can't be found,
If people wish. Consider gold
And silver, riches manifold
And precious; yet they make the price
For adultery and other vice.
Good weapons human peace maintain,
And yet with them good men are slain
Unlawfully in all the lands
Where robbers hold them in their hands.

46. The Nightingale is trying to use the same justification for her song as the Owl. The latter claimed that she forewarned, but could not be blamed for what she foresaw (ll. 1233–58): the Nightingale, having admitted that she sings where ladies and lovely girls throng (l. 1338), exculpates herself from the consequences of her song.

These instances are like my song,
Which tends to virtue. Taken wrong,
It may lead people to transgress
And do all kinds of foolishness.
But must you, wretch, speak ill of love,
The purest thing, by heaven above,
That ever man and woman know
Unless it's stolen? Then it's low,
Impure, corrupt and wholly dross.
May the anger of the Holy Cross
Rend those who break the natural law!
The wonder with them is that more
Don't lose their wits. They're mad at best
Who go to brood without a nest.
Woman's flesh is soft and frail
And carnal lusts – alas! – prevail;
No wonder then that they persist
And women find they can't resist.
And yet they are not wholly lost
Who at the jump of lust are tossed:
For many women rise again
And leave the mire in which they've lain.
Nor are their vices all the same;[47]
There are two different kinds of shame.
One springs from flesh's lusty fire,
The other from spiritual desire.

47. Ironically, the poet puts the description of the Seven Deadly Sins into the mouth of the Nightingale. They are all clear except two. 'Joy at others' sinful plight' is Envy. The Nightingale, somewhat unorthodox in her suggestion that sins of the flesh are less serious than those of the spirit, puts her finger on the Owl's weakness, pride.

The flesh leads man to drunkenness,
To laziness and wantonness.
The spirit leads to rage and spite
And joy at others' sinful plight.
For more and more it strives apace
And doesn't care for mercy and grace,
Then rearing up in haughty show,
It proudly scorns what lies below.
Now tell me, which shall have your curse,
Flesh or spirit? Which is worse?
You may answer if you wish
That flesh is far less devilish,
For many a man is pure of flesh
Whose spirit's in the devil's mesh.
No man should censure with disgust
A woman for her fleshly lust,
For he who from her turns aside
Commits the greater sin of pride.
But if to love I chance to bring
A wife or virgin when I sing,
Then I defend the virgin's cause;
And if you'd understand my laws,
Listen with an attentive ear,
And I shall make my reasons clear.
If a girl loves secretly
She trips and falls at Nature's plea,
And though she frolic many a day
She hasn't gone too far astray.
The Church may bring her back to good
When she atones her lustihood.
Indeed she well may wed the man
She loved – which none would wish to scan.

231

Then she can love him in the light
Who used to steal to her by night.
A young girl hardly knows her way;
By youthful blood she's led astray.
Some lout entices her to sin
By every trick he's expert in.
He'll come and go, command, then plead,
Possess her, and then pay no heed.
Her sighs are frequent, loud and long:
Treated like this, she must go wrong!
She's never known what life's about,
And so she must at last find out,
And closely learn to play the game
That makes a girl's high spirits tame.
And when I see the drawn, strained face
With which love clouds that youthful grace,
In pity I am bound to sing
To cheer her out of suffering.
I teach these youngsters with my song
That love like that does not last long.
It merely brushes with its wing,
Then goes, just like the song I sing.
Such girls discover it soon departs,
And calm returns to aching hearts.
I still sing with them, even so;
Beginning high and ending low,
I gently let my music fall
Until it makes no sound at all.
Girls know, who hear that ending sigh,
That love, like song, is quick to die.
A brief excitement, like a breath,
That quickly lives and has its death.

Through me a girl can understand,
And wisdom comes at her command.
She clearly gathers from my song
That dizzy love does not last long.
But one thing I assert to you:
I hate it when a wife's untrue.
A wife should note I never sing
At times when I am carrying.[48]
She must, though marriage bonds seem hard,
Pay fools' words utter disregard.
To me it is a dreadful case
When any man so falls from grace
That lusting passion grips his life,
And he must do his neighbour's wife.
One of two things comes from the act;
There is no third, and that's a fact.
The husband's either strong and brave,
Or feeble, like a worthless slave.
Now, if he's honourable and brave,
No man of sense would so behave
As to disgrace him through his wife.
He'd stand in danger of his life,
Or payment of that penalty
Which from his lust will set him free.[49]

48. See note 20. Here, the Nightingale by implication advocates a close season for sexual activity during pregnancy, a time likely to produce masculine infidelity.

49. 'There is evidence in the thirteenth century that the out-raged husband who found his wife in the act of adultery was no longer allowed to slay the guilty pair or either of them, but was allowed to emasculate the adulterer.' (E. G. Stanley, op. cit., who cites Pollock and Maitland, *History of English Law*, 2nd edn, (Cambridge, 1898).)

And even if he's not in terror
It is a wicked, senseless error
To harm a worthy man like this
And steal away his marriage bliss.
But if she has a worthless lord,
Feeble in bed, feeble at board,
Whose churlish belly lays her flat,
How can he love her after that?
His passion cannot rise too high
When such a fellow gropes her thigh.
Now from the first act comes disgrace;
The second one is merely base;
And both adulteries are grave.
For if the husband's strong and brave,
When you're lying with his wife
You well might tremble for your life.
And if the husband's only scum,
What pleasure from the deed will come?
You think of who last slaked her lust,
And pay her favour with disgust.
A decent fellow, after this,
Would hardly seek with her his bliss.
If he but thought with whom she lay,
His love would quickly fade away.'

      The Owl was glad to hear this tale
Because she thought the Nightingale,
Whose speech at first she had admired,
Had at the finish quite misfired,
And so she said: 'Young girls, I find,
Most fill your charitable mind.
You sympathize and take their side,
And overpraise them far and wide.

The married women turn to me,
And bring their woes, whatever they be,
For often difference or dissension
In man and wife arouse contention;
And that man leads a guilty life
Who loves to poke another's wife,
And gives his wealth and love away
To a woman who cannot repay,
Leaving at home his lawful spouse –
All bare the walls, empty the house.
He leaves her starved, with little to wear,
Cupboard empty, clothes threadbare.
And when he comes back home at last
His wife must keep her mouth shut fast,
For all that he brings home is bad.
He yells and storms at her like mad;
Whatever she does makes him shout,
And if she speaks, it puts him out.
And often when she's saintliest
He slams her teeth in with his fist:
A man is bound to make her loose
To whom he offers such abuse.
Ill-treated by such constant spite,
She'll sometime take her own delight;
And if she cuckolds him, God knows,
It's not her fault the case arose.
It often happens the wife is sweet
And tender, with a figure neat,
And fair complexion, a delight
Which makes still worse the man's despite –
To chase a slut who's worth much less
Than one hair from his own wife's tress!

And since such men are everywhere,
Wives pure in thought and deed are rare.
Such men are jealous, full of fear[50]
That if their wives give courteous ear
And pleasant talk to other men,
Their marriage will be broken then.
Behind locked doors their wives are shut,
And that's how marriage bonds get cut.
For if they're held in this subjection
Their actions take a new direction.
Cursed be the man who talks too much
When wives revenge themselves on such!
Of these things wives to me complain;
They make me sad and give me pain.
My heart is almost broken when
I see them suffer through their men.
For them my salt tears fall apace;
I pray to Christ to grant them grace,
To cure their woes and make them true,
And send them better husbands too.
     'And now I'll tell you one thing more.
You'll find no answer, I am sure,
To save your skin, and this debate
With your defeat will terminate.
Many a merchant, many a knight,
Loves and clasps his wife aright,

50. Like the Owl's acceptance of adultery when the husband
deserves to be cuckolded (l. 1543), and her call to Christ to grant
his grace to the cuckolding wives (ll. 1568–70), this condemnation of jealousy provides evidence of a liberal position on her
part.

And many a country husband too;
And so the wife stays good and true
In bed, and serves him well at board,
With gentle deed and kindly word.
And eagerly she strives to please
By doing things that give him ease.
The lord goes off to work to win
A livelihood, which brings them in
Their needs. The wife most sadly grieves
Every time her husband leaves
On anxious journeys; longingly
She sighs and sits in misery,
And for her absent husband's sake
Spends days in care and nights awake.
And time seems long this weary while;
To her, each step becomes a mile.
Around her, sleep embraces all;
Alone, I listen by the wall,
For well I know her aching heart.
I sing at night to take her part,
And that my song may bring relief,
I tune it partly to her grief.
Because I share her misery
The doleful lady welcomes me.
I do my best to help such wives
Who strive for virtue all their lives.

     'You've put me in such furious heat
My heart has almost ceased to beat,
And I can hardly speak. But still
I'll press my charge with all my will.
You say I fill all men with hate
And that in anger, soon and late,

They set on me with sticks and stones
And batter me and break my bones.
And when through this I come to die,
Upon the hedge they hang me high
To scare the magpie and the crow
From fields where men have been to sow.
And though it's true, I do them good,
Because for men I shed my blood.
To them my death brings benefit,
Something yours will scarce permit.
For when you're dead, dried up and small,
Your body can't be used at all.
I cannot think what good you bring,
You're such a wretched, useless thing.
But when the life's shot out of me,
I still have some utility.
I can be stuck upon a stick
In woodlands where the boughs grow thick
To help the hunters lure, then snatch,
The little birds they like to catch.
And so man's diet is complete:
I help them to their roasted meat.
Alive or dead, you're just the same;
What human service can you claim?
I don't know why you rear a brood;
Alive or dead, they bring no good.'

      The Nightingale heard this doom,
And hopping on a twig in bloom,
She perched still higher than before.
'Owl,' she said, 'Hear still some more!
I'll cease to plead since your renown
And speaking skill have let you down.

Men rage at you, you say. You boast
They hate you to the uttermost;
With yells and mournful howls you burst,
Complaining that you are accurst.
Boys capture you, and then are quick
To hoist you high upon a stick
And rip you into bits, or make
A scarecrow of you on a stake.
You boast of these, but lose the game,
Because such things bring only shame.
In bragging of your own disgrace,
You grant to me the winner's place.'
      And having uttered this reply,
Into a lovely spot nearby
She flew, and tuned her voice to sing,
Then trilled in such sweet carolling
Her song was heard both far and near.
The thrush and mavis came to hear,[51]
The woodpecker and oriole,
Birds small and great, all glad of soul
Because the Nightingale, none doubted,
Had trounced the Owl; and so they shouted,
Then sang so many melodies
That bliss was there among the trees.
When gamblers lose, it's just the same;
Men jeer at them, they're put to shame.
On hearing this, the Owl cried out,
'Did you call up this warring rout,

51. Gatherings of birds often figure in medieval literature. They gather to debate, to resolve disputes, to witness duels, to acclaim victors. Atkins (*The Owl and the Nightingale*, Cambridge U.P. 1922) has a full and useful note on this poet's use of the convention, and describes other examples.

You wretch! D'you want to pick a fight?
No, no! You haven't half the might.
Why do they shout, these at your back?
I think you lead them to attack.
But you shall learn before you fly
What strength we have, my kind and I.
For birds with claws all sharp and bent
And great hooked beaks for tearing meant
Are my relations, all of whom,
If I requested help, would come.
The cock himself, a worthy knight,[52]
Would take my side in any fight,
Because beneath the welkin we
Both sing aloud nocturnally.
If I should raise the hue and cry,
So huge a host with me would fly,
Your pride would surely have a fall.
I wouldn't give a turd for you all.
By night there wouldn't be a feather
Left on all of you together.
But we decided, did we not,
When we came here to this spot,
That we'd abide by the decision
Our judge arrived at with precision?
And will you now go back on it?
To law, it seems you won't submit,
But since you fear to lose the case,
You offer battle, you disgrace!

52. One of the earliest references to the fighting qualities of the
cock. Whether it is coincidence or not, the first reference to actual
cock-fighting in English is in the *Life of St Thomas* written by
William Fitzstephen, who died in 1190.

Yet this advice I give you all
Before the hue and cry I call:
Give up your plan to have a fight
And very quickly take to flight,
For by my talons sharp and fine,
If you await this force of mine,
I fear you'll sing another tune,
And curse all fighting very soon.
There's not a bird among you all
My battle mask would not appal.'

    Thus boldly spoke the Owl, for though
She did not mean to visit woe
On them by calling up her host,
Yet all the same it pleased her most[53]
To threaten thus the Nightingale,
For many a man of no avail
With point of spear and thrust of shield,
Who's feeble on the battlefield,
Can make his foeman sweat with fear
With valiant words and looks severe.

    Soon after in the morning then,
Because she sang so well, the Wren[54]
Arrived to help the Nightingale,
For though her form and voice were frail,
She sang out shrill in perfect measure,
And with her song gave men much pleasure.

53. The state of mind of the Owl here described, together with the poet's comment, is like that of the Nightingale at lines 1067–1074.

54. The Wren obtains the respect appropriate to one who, though the smallest of birds, was acknowledged King. (See Introduction, p. 169 n.)

She was considered wise, the Wren,
Having been reared in realms of men.
From them she'd got her canny head:
She was not in the woodlands bred.
And she would speak out, I declare,
Before the king, or anywhere.

      'Listen!' she said, 'and mark my speech!
The king will know if it you breach
His peace and bring his realm to shame;
For he is neither dead nor lame.
You two shall suffer harm and stain
If you break peace in his domain.
So be less hostile, I entreat,
And let us to the judgement seat;
And there the verdict shall indeed
End all debate, as was agreed.'

      'I'm willing,' said the Nightingale,
'But not because your words prevail.
No, Wren, my sense of law it is
That makes me hope injustices
Will never win. My fearless trust
I place in verdicts that are just.
I still maintain my solemn gage
That Master Nicholas, our sage,
Shall judge the case between us two,
And that is what I hope he'll do.
Where shall we find the wise man then?'

      'What! Don't you know?' exclaimed the Wren
From where she sat on a sprig of lime,
'At Portisham,[55] this present time.

55. Portisham still exists, a small village on the sea side of a
ridge not far from Dorchester. It has a small partly Norman
church which once belonged to the monastery at Abbotsbury.

Upon an outlet, near the sea,
In Dorsetshire: there sojourns he.
And there he gives his judgements out,
His writings and his sayings devout.
And from the wisdom he transmits,
Even Scotland benefits.
To find him is most easily done:
His living is a single one,
And to the bishops that's a shame,
As well as to all who know his name,
His wisdom, calling and career.
If they would use him, it is clear
His presence, with his wise advice
Would benefit them – and the price?
A spread of livings so that he
Could often at their service be.'

    'Yes,' said the Owl, 'I think the same.
And these great men are much to blame
Ignoring one of such good sense,
Such power of mind and excellence.
They give out livings in a stream,
But he is held in low esteem.
They're kinder to their families:
Their babies get incumbencies.[56]
Their sense should tell them they were wrong,
Neglecting Nicholas so long.
Our pros and cons all being trim,
It's time we took our case to him.'

    'Agreed!' the Nightingale replied,
'But who shall be our legal guide,

56. A common abuse of ecclesiastical and secular power.
Henry II made his own bastard, a youth not come of age, Bishop
of London (see Introduction, p. 160).

And plead before the judgement seat?'
    'This difficulty I can meet,'
The Owl replied. 'For I can say
Every word you've heard today,[57]
And if you think that I go wrong,
Object, and make your protest strong.'
        And having thus both said their say,
Without their troops they took their way
To Portisham. But how they fared
In judgement when their case was aired
I cannot tell: it all depends.
For this is where my story ends.

57. A final surprise. The poet accords the Owl the power of perfect memorization, one of the highest graces a scholar of divinity could possess. It was thought to be a special gift of God to those likely to use its means to enlighten mankind.

APPENDIX
AND
BIBLIOGRAPHY

APPENDIX

Matters Relating to the Manuscripts, Authors and Dates of the Poems

'ST ERKENWALD' is preserved in a single manuscript, Brit. Mus. Harl.2250, f. 72b–75a (Gollancz, *St Erkenwald*, London, 1922). The manuscript, which contains miscellaneous and mainly religious poetry, is dated 1477 by the scribe who copied it, but linguistic and other evidence places the composition of the poem in the late fourteenth century. It seems that most commentators have followed Gollancz in assuming the poem to be the work of the 'Pearl' poet, but the linguistic and stylistic evidence do not appear to me conclusive. Although Gollancz puts the poem after 'Cleanness' and 'Patience' in the poet's development, he acknowledges that 'its diction is simpler than that of those poems, it lacks their strength and intensity; but this sign of weakness might be due to its being composed for some special occasion, and not a theme chosen by the poet and slowly elaborated. If not the work of the poet of "Patience" and "Cleanness," "Erkenwald" must be due to some disciple who very cleverly caught the style of his master' (p. lvii). John Gardner (*The Complete Works of the Gawain-Poet,* University of Chicago, 1965, p. 342) inclines to support Gollancz and Savage (whose advocacy of the 'Pearl' poet's authorship is set forth in *Yale Studies in English*, vol. LXXII, 1926, pp. xxxi–lxv) and suggests that 'all who have worked most closely with' the poems agree. He states: 'The similarity of themes, images and attitudes will be obvious to every reader. The conclusive argument, when it comes, will probably be based upon metrical considerations, for only one poet whose work has come down to us handles rhythms in the way they are handled here. The hypothesis of a clever imitator of "Sir Gawain and the Green Knight" simply will not wash.' But Larry D. Benson (*Journal of English and German Philology*, vol. 64, July 1965, pp. 393–405), reviewing scholarly progress in the matter, notes that the number of strict stylistic parallels between 'St Erkenwald' and the other poems mentioned reduces with each survey that is made; there are now only five, he says, and asks what is left if the stylistic evidence for the theory of common authorship has gone. The alliterative metre itself and the common techniques of medieval story-telling, with its rhetorical exhortations, its appeals to previous authority, and its stock phrases, did indeed provide a frame within which all poets worked; therefore more certain evidence is required before the poem is finally assigned to the 'Pearl' poet. My own opinion – for I too have now worked closely with all five of the poems in the group – is that three pieces of evidence have been omitted, which may be added to those Gollancz supplies (op. cit. p. lvi) in support of his opinion. One is the extraordinary harmony of pattern which emerges from a close study of the five poems; this really seems to me to be the distinct creative quality of a single poet (see my introductions to 'St Erkenwald' and 'Cleanness' in this volume, to 'Sir Gawain and the Green Knight', and to 'Pearl' and 'Patience' in *Medieval English Verse*, Penguin, 1964, pp. 136 and 118). The second is the brevity and force of the ending, which is a rare quality in a verbose age; whether the ending is consolatory, as in 'Sir Gawain' and 'Pearl', expository and admonitory as in 'Patience' and 'Cleanness', or celebratory, as in 'St Erkenwald', the relevance and economy are admirable. And the third piece of evidence is the doctrinal precision of each theme treated in the five poems.

'CLEANNESS' figures, together with 'Pearl', 'Patience', and 'Sir Gawain and the Green Knight', on the single late-fourteenth-century manuscript Cotton Nero A.x, which is in the British Museum. 'Cleanness' occurs second. There is general agreement that all the poems are by the same unknown author, being in the same north-western dialect and broadly the same style, as well as having a wide range of resemblances in choice and treatment of themes, characterization and form. There are two illustrations of 'Cleanness' on the manuscript, which are in an inferior style, and of later date than the writing of the poem. One shows Noah and his family in an open boat, and the other represents Daniel expounding to Belshazzar and his queen; behind the agitated king the disembodied hand has just completed the Writing on the Wall.

In translating and editing the poem I have followed Gollancz in his quatrain and division arrangements, except where I have noted a difference. On the manuscript the main divisions of the poem are indicated by the placing, at the beginning of the sections, of big, elaborate initial letters in blue flourished with red, extending through eight lines; and the sub-divisions similarly, though the letters are smaller, extending through three lines.

Though the irregularity of the poem's structure has been commented on repeatedly, I find that the increasing length and complexity of the three sections – which run to 556, 600 and 656 lines respectively – and the knitting together of the parts, make up a most harmonious artefact.

'THE OWL AND THE NIGHTINGALE' survives in two manuscripts, MS Cotton Caligula A.ix, and MS Jesus College 29. The former is in the British Museum and the latter in the Bodleian, and they are usually referred to, respectively, as (C) and (J). (C) is considered to have been written in the first half of the thirteenth century, and the relevant part of (J) perhaps half a century later. The date of composition is thought to be between 1189, when Henry II died, and 1216, when Henry III came to the throne (see ll. 1091–2 and note). Discussion of the possible authorship has generally revolved round the name of the proposed judge of the two birds, Nicholas of Guildford. Miss K. Huganir (*The Owl and the Nightingale: Sources, Date, Author* Haskell 1931) supports his candidacy, and is surprisingly followed by J. A. W. Bennett and G. V. Smithers, who give the poem in full in their selection, *Early Middle English Verse and Prose*, Oxford, 1966. They think it must be Nicholas of Guildford and say that the 'humorous hyperbole of the assertion that he has spread sweetness and light all over England makes it easy to accept the self-advertisement'. But E. G. Stanley, who summarizes the authorship debate on pp. 20–21 of his introduction to the poem is surely right when he states: 'The reason for doubting that Nicholas is the author is in the poet's charge that Nicholas's superiors abuse their power and corruptly and nepotistically make over the emoluments from ecclesiastical offices to those unfit to discharge them.' The reference is to lines 1761–79, which seem to indicate that the poem was written on behalf of Nicholas rather than by him. In view of the large number of clerics named Nicholas found in twelfth-century records, none of whom appear to have been connected with Portisham, only fresh evidence is likely to throw any light on the circumstances of the poem's composition or the identity of the author. I may mention in an only half-serious aside, that dissolute clerics were often called Nicholas, like the uproarious 'hende Nicholas' in Chaucer's 'The Miller's Tale'. St Nicholas was the patron saint of scholars and parish clerks: possibly the survival from early Germanic tongues of words like *nicker* ('sea-monster' in Anglo-Saxon, 'water-wraith' in Scandinavian folklore and 'goblin' in German) helped on the association between the name Nicholas and unnatural naughtiness. Eventually Old Nick became the devil's own name – but that was much later, and partly consequent upon Machiavelli's first name being Niccolò.

BIBLIOGRAPHY

Texts

St Erkenwald, ed. Sir I. Gollancz, Early English Text Society,
Oxford, 1922

St Erkenwald, ed. Henry L. Savage, Yale U.P., 1926

Cleanness, ed. Sir I. Gollancz, Early English Text Society,
Oxford, 1921

Cleanness in Pearl, Cleanness, Patience, Sir Gawain and the
Green Knight, ed. A. C. Cawley and J. J. Anderson,
Dent, Everyman's Library, 1976

Purity (Cleanness), ed. R. J. Menner, Yale Studies LXI, New
Haven, 1920

The Owl and the Nightingale, ed. J. W. H. Atkins, Cambridge
U.P., 1922

The Owl and the Nightingale, ed. J. H. G. Grattan and G. F. H.
Sykes, Early English Text Society, Oxford U.P., 1935

The Owl and the Nightingale, ed. E. G. Stanley, Nelson,
1960

The Owl and the Nightingale, ed. J. E. Wells, Heath, 1907

Study Articles

St Erkenwald

Benson L. D., Journal of English and German Philology, vol. 64,
July 1965, pp. 393–405

Savage H. L., Yale Studies in English, vol. LXXII, 1926, pp.
xxi–lxv

Cleanness

Bateson H., Modern Language Review, vol. 19, January 1924,
pp. 95–101

Brewer D. S., Essays in Criticism, vol. 17, April 1967, pp. 130–
42

Ebbs J. D., Journal of English and German Philology, vol. 57, July 1958, pp.622–5

The Owl and the Nightingale

Atkins J. W. H., Aberystwyth Studies 4, 1922, pp. 49–58

Baldwin A. W., 'Henry II and The Owl and the Nightingale' in *English and German Philology*, vol. 66, April 1967, pp. 207–9

Carson M. A., 'Rhetorical Structure in The Owl and the Nightingale' in *Speculum*, vol. 42, January 1967, pp. 92–103

Donovan M., 'The Owl as Religious Altruist' in *Medieval Studies*, XVIII, 1956, pp. 207–14.

Cawley A. C., 'Astrology in The Owl and the Nightingale' in *Modern Language Review*, vol. 46, 1962, pp. 161–74

Coulton G. G., *Modern Language Review*, vol. 17, 1922, pp. 69–71

Gottschalk J., 'Lay Preachers to a Lay Audience' in *Philological Quarterly*, vol. 45, October 1966, pp. 657–67

Hinckley H. B., Publications of the Modern Language Association of America, vol. 44, 1929, pp. 69–71; vol. 46, 1931, pp. 93–101; vol. 47, 1947, pp. 303–14

Kinneavy G. B., 'Fortune, Providence and the Owl' in *Studies in Philology*, vol. 64, October 1964, pp. 655–64

Lumiansky R. N., 'Concerning The Owl and the Nightingale' in *Philological Quarterly*, vol. 32, 1953, pp. 411–17

Russell J. C., 'The Patrons of The Owl and the Nightingale', in *Philological Quarterly*, vol. 47, April 1969, no. 2., pp. 178–85

Sisam C., *Review of English Studies*, vol. 13, November 1962, pp. 143–6

Stanley E. G., *English and German Studies*, vol. 6, 1957, pp. 30–63

(N.B. E. G. Stanley gives a fuller list of study articles, up to 1960, in his edition of *The Owl and the Nightingale*.)

Literary and Critical

Anderson M. N., *Drama and Imagery in Medieval English Churches*, Cambridge U.P., 1963

BIBLIOGRAPHY

Atkins J. W. H., *English Literary Criticism: The Medieval Phase*, Methuen, 1943

Bennet J. A. W., and Smithers G. V. (ed.), *Early Middle English Verse and Prose*, Oxford U.P., 1966

Bethurum D. (ed.), *Critical Approaches to Medieval Literature*, Columbia U.P., 1960

Bloomfield M. W., *The Seven Deadly Sins*, Michigan State U.P., 1952

Everett D., *Essays on Middle English Literature* (ed. Kean P.), Oxford U.P., 1955

Gardner J., *The Complete Works of the Gawain-Poet*, Chicago U.P., 1965

Huganir K., *The Owl and the Nightingale: Sources, Date, Author* Haskell, 1931

Lewis C. S., *The Allegory of Love*, Oxford U.P., 1936

Lewis C. S., *The Discarded Image*, Cambridge U.P., 1964

Mandeville, Sir J., *Travels*, ed. Malcolm Letts, Hakluyt Society, 1954

Moorman C., *The Pearl-Poet*, Twayne, 1968

Oakden J. P., *Alliterative Poetry in Middle English*, Manchester U.P., 1930

Robertson D. W. Jr., *A Preface to Chaucer*, Princeton U.P., 1962

Robinson F. M., ed. *Poems of Geoffrey Chaucer*, Houghton Mifflin, 1933

Spiers J., *Medieval English Poetry*, Faber, 1957

Stone, B., *Sir Gawain and the Green Knight*, Penguin, 2nd edn, 1974

Stone B., *Medieval English Verse*, Penguin, 1964

Waddell H., *The Wandering Scholars*, 7th edn. revised, Constable, 1934

White T. H., *The Book of Beasts*, Cape, 1954

Wilson R. M., *Early Middle English Literature*, Methuen, 1939

Historical

Bede, *A History of the English Church and People*, 731 (trans. Leo Sherley-Price), Penguin, 1965

Coulton G. G., *Medieval Panorama*, Cambridge, 1938

Dugdale, Sir W., *A History of St Paul's Cathedral (1658)* with additions by H. Ellis, Lackington, 1818

Geoffrey of Monmouth, *The History of the Kings of Britain*, (trans. Lewis Thorpe), Penguin, 1966

Heer F., *The Medieval World*, Weidenfeld & Nicolson, 1962

Matthews W. R. and Atkins W. M., *A History of St Paul's Cathedral*, Baker, 1957

Wheeler Sir R. M. W., *London and the Saxons*, London Museum Catalogue No. 6, 1935

Whitelock D., *The Beginnings of English Society*, Pelican, 1952

Reference

Bradley H. (ed.), *Stratmann's Middle English Dictionary*, Oxford, 1891

Brewer, Rev. E. Cobham, *A Dictionary of Phrase and Fable*, Cassell, undated

Shipley J. T. (ed.), *Dictionary of World Literary Terms*, Allen & Unwin, 1955

The Dictionary of National Biography

The Jewish Encyclopaedia

The New Catholic Encyclopaedia

SELECTIVE INDEX

FOR THE BEST IN PAPERBACKS, LOOK FOR THE ⊕

In every corner of the world, on every subject under the sun, Penguin represents quality and variety – the very best in publishing today.

For complete information about books available from Penguin – including Pelicans, Puffins, Peregrines and Penguin Classics – and how to order them, write to us at the appropriate address below. Please note that for copyright reasons the selection of books varies from country to country.

In the United Kingdom: For a complete list of books available from Penguin in the U.K., please write to *Dept E.P., Penguin Books Ltd, Harmondsworth, Middlesex, UB7 0DA*

In the United States: For a complete list of books available from Penguin in the U.S., please write to *Dept BA, Penguin, 299 Murray Hill Parkway, East Rutherford, New Jersey 07073*

In Canada: For a complete list of books available from Penguin in Canada, please write to *Penguin Books Canada Ltd, 2801 John Street, Markham, Ontario L3R 1B4*

In Australia: For a complete list of books available from Penguin in Australia, please write to the *Marketing Department, Penguin Books Australia Ltd, P.O. Box 257, Ringwood, Victoria 3134*

In New Zealand: For a complete list of books available from Penguin in New Zealand, please write to the *Marketing Department, Penguin Books (NZ) Ltd, Private Bag, Takapuna, Auckland 9*

In India: For a complete list of books available from Penguin, please write to *Penguin Overseas Ltd, 706 Eros Apartments, 56 Nehru Place, New Delhi, 110019*

In Holland: For a complete list of books available from Penguin in Holland, please write to *Penguin Books Nederland B.V., Postbus 195, NL–1380AD Weesp, Netherlands*

In Germany: For a complete list of books available from Penguin, please write to *Penguin Books Ltd, Friedrichstrasse 10 – 12, D–6000 Frankfurt Main 1, Federal Republic of Germany*

In Spain: For a complete list of books available from Penguin in Spain, please write to *Longman Penguin España, Calle San Nicolas 15, E–28013 Madrid, Spain*

PENGUIN CLASSICS

FOR THE BEST IN PAPERBACKS, LOOK FOR THE 🐧

PENGUIN CLASSICS

Benjamin Disraeli	**Sybil**
George Eliot	**Adam Bede**
	Daniel Deronda
	Felix Holt
	Middlemarch
	The Mill on the Floss
	Romola
	Scenes of Clerical Life
	Silas Marner
Elizabeth Gaskell	**Cranford** and **Cousin Phillis**
	The Life of Charlotte Brontë
	Mary Barton
	North and South
	Wives and Daughters
Edward Gibbon	**The Decline and Fall of the Roman Empire**
George Gissing	**New Grub Street**
Edmund Gosse	**Father and Son**
Richard Jefferies	**Landscape with Figures**
Thomas Macaulay	**The History of England**
Henry Mayhew	**Selections from London Labour** and **The London Poor**
John Stuart Mill	**On Liberty**
William Morris	**News from Nowhere** and **Selected Writings and Designs**
Walter Pater	**Marius the Epicurean**
John Ruskin	**'Unto This Last' and Other Writings**
Sir Walter Scott	**Ivanhoe**
Robert Louis Stevenson	**Dr Jekyll and Mr Hyde**
William Makepeace Thackeray	**The History of Henry Esmond**
	Vanity Fair
Anthony Trollope	**Barchester Towers**
	Framley Parsonage
	Phineas Finn
	The Warden
Mrs Humphrey Ward	**Helbeck of Bannisdale**
Mary Wollstonecraft	**Vindication of the Rights of Woman**

Arnold Bennett	**The Old Wives' Tale**
Joseph Conrad	**Heart of Darkness**
	Nostromo
	The Secret Agent
	The Shadow-Line
	Under Western Eyes
E. M. Forster	**Howard's End**
	A Passage to India
	A Room With a View
	Where Angels Fear to Tread
Thomas Hardy	**The Distracted Preacher and Other Tales**
	Far From the Madding Crowd
	Jude the Obscure
	The Mayor of Casterbridge
	The Return of the Native
	Tess of the d'Urbervilles
	The Trumpet Major
	Under the Greenwood Tree
	The Woodlanders
Henry James	**The Aspern Papers** and **The Turn of the Screw**
	The Bostonians
	Daisy Miller
	The Europeans
	The Golden Bowl
	An International Episode and Other Stories
	Portrait of a Lady
	Roderick Hudson
	Washington Square
	What Maisie Knew
	The Wings of the Dove
D. H. Lawrence	**The Complete Short Novels**
	The Plumed Serpent
	The Rainbow
	Selected Short Stories
	Sons and Lovers
	The White Peacock
	Women in Love

FOR THE BEST IN PAPERBACKS, LOOK FOR THE 🐧

PENGUIN CLASSICS

Netochka Nezvanova   Fyodor Dostoyevsky

Dostoyevsky's first book tells the story of 'Nameless Nobody' and introduces many of the themes and issues which will dominate his great masterpieces.

Selections from the Carmina Burana   A verse translation by David Parlett

The famous songs from the *Carmina Burana* (made into an oratorio by Carl Orff) tell of lecherous monks and corrupt clerics, drinkers and gamblers, and the fleeting pleasures of youth.

Fear and Trembling   Søren Kierkegaard

A profound meditation on the nature of faith and submission to God's will which examines with startling originality the story of Abraham and Isaac.

Selected Prose   Charles Lamb

Lamb's famous essays (under the strange pseudonym of Elia) on anything and everything have long been celebrated for their apparently innocent charm; this major new edition allows readers to discover the darker and more interesting aspects of Lamb.

The Picture of Dorian Gray   Oscar Wilde

Wilde's superb and macabre novella, one of his supreme works, is reprinted here with a masterly Introduction and valuable Notes by Peter Ackroyd.

A Treatise of Human Nature   David Hume

A universally acknowledged masterpiece by 'the greatest of all British Philosophers' – A. J. Ayer

FOR THE BEST IN PAPERBACKS, LOOK FOR THE

PENGUIN CLASSICS

A Passage to India E. M. Forster

Centred on the unresolved mystery in the Marabar Caves, Forster's great work provides the definitive evocation of the British Raj.

The Republic Plato

The best-known of Plato's dialogues, *The Republic* is also one of the supreme masterpieces of Western philosophy whose influence cannot be overestimated.

The Life of Johnson James Boswell

Perhaps the finest 'life' ever written, Boswell's *Johnson* captures for all time one of the most colourful and talented figures in English literary history.

Remembrance of Things Past (3 volumes) Marcel Proust

This revised version by Terence Kilmartin of C. K. Scott Moncrieff's original translation has been universally acclaimed – available for the first time in paperback.

Metamorphoses Ovid

A golden treasury of myths and legends which has proved a major influence on Western literature.

A Nietzsche Reader Friedrich Nietzsche

A superb selection from all the major works of one of the greatest thinkers and writers in world literature, translated into clear, modern English.

PENGUIN CLASSICS

Aeschylus	**The Oresteia** **(Agamemnon/Choephori/Eumenides)** **Prometheus Bound/The Suppliants/Seven** **Against Thebes/The Persians**
Aesop	**Fables**
Apollonius of Rhodes	**The Voyage of Argo**
Apuleius	**The Golden Ass**
Aristophanes	**The Knights/Peace/The Birds/The Assembly** **Women/Wealth**
	Lysistrata/The Acharnians/The Clouds/
	The Wasps/The Poet and the Women/The Frogs
Aristotle	**The Athenian Constitution**
	The Ethics
	The Politics
Aristotle/Horace/	
Longinus	**Classical Literary Criticism**
Arrian	**The Campaigns of Alexander**
Saint Augustine	**City of God**
	Confessions
Boethius	**The Consolation of Philosophy**
Caesar	**The Civil War**
	The Conquest of Gaul
Catullus	**Poems**
Cicero	**The Murder Trials**
	The Nature of the Gods
	On the Good Life
	Selected Letters
	Selected Political Speeches
	Selected Works
Euripides	**Alcestis/Iphigenia in Tauris/Hippolytus/The** **Bacchae/Ion/The Women of Troy/Helen**
	Medea/Hecabe/Electra/Heracles

	Orestes/The Children of Heracles/
	    Andromache/The Suppliant Woman/
	    The Phoenician Women/Iphigenia in Aulis